A DISCOVERY: *love* & OTHER THINGS

VICTORIA WOODS

A STEAM-Y NOVEL

Victoria Woods

A Discovery: Love and Other Things Copyright © 2023 by Victoria Woods

All rights reserved.

First Edition.

ISBN: 979-8-9863562-5-9

This is a work of fiction. All characters, places, businesses, and events in this novel may reflect actual characters, places, businesses, and events but are used in a fictional manner. Any resemblance to actual persons, living or dead, actual places, or actual events are purely coincidental. No part of this work may be reproduced in any form without written consent of the author.

Cover Design:
Sam Palencia, https://www.inkandlaurel.com/

Interior Formatting and Illustrations:
Brian Ladlee, https://www.brianladlee.com/

Editing:
Paisley Prophet, https://www.fiverr.com/p_prophet

Proofreading:
Nisha Ladlee, https://www.passionauthorservices.com/

For mature audiences only.

Table of Contents

For all the children of immigrants who spend their lives struggling to connect with their motherlands…you belong.

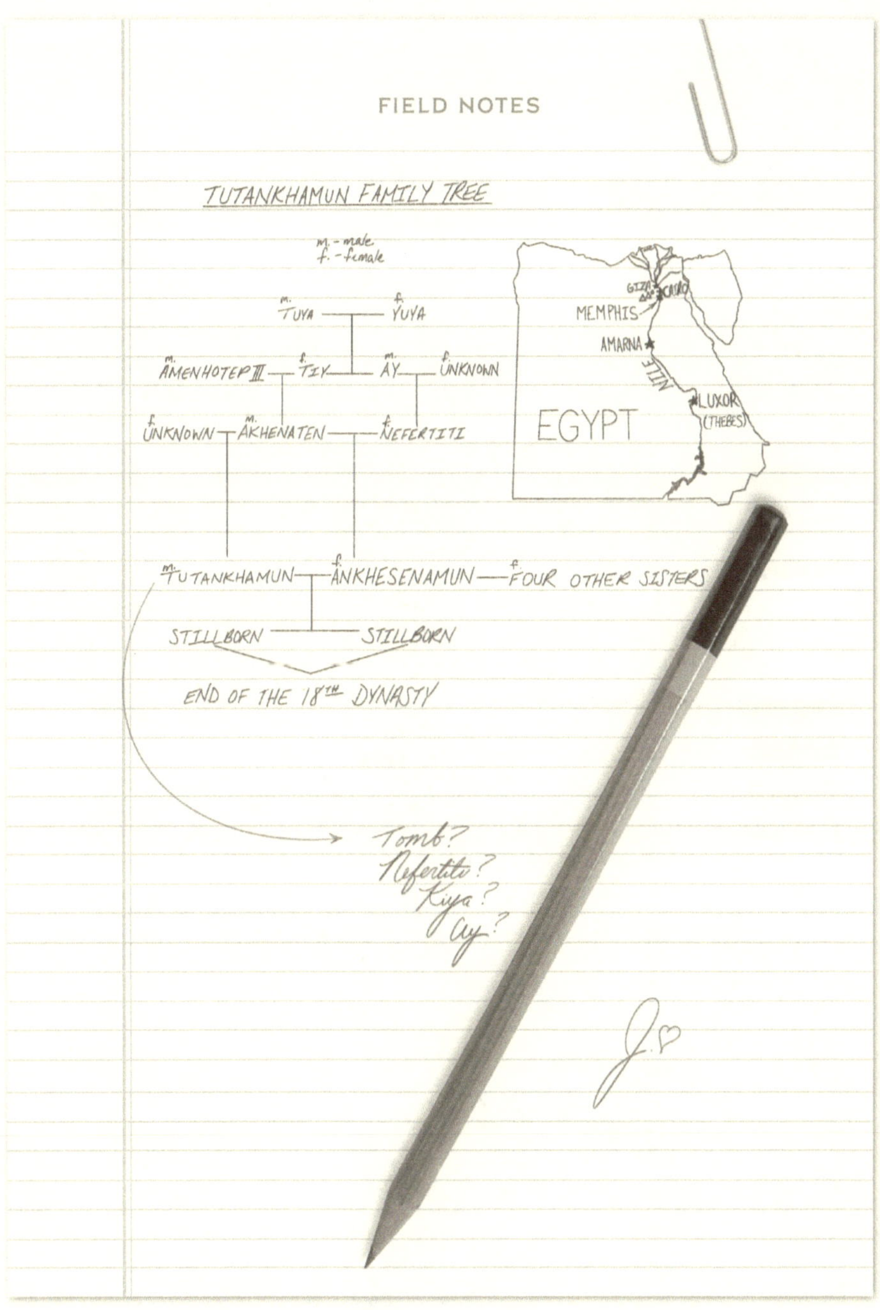
FIELD NOTES
TUTANKHAMUN FAMILY TREE
m. - male
f. - female
m. TUYA
f. YUYA
m. AMENHOTEP III
f. TIY
m. AY
f. UNKNOWN
f. UNKNOWN
m. AKHENATEN
f. NEFERTITI
m. TUTANKHAMUN
f. ANKHESENAMUN
f. FOUR OTHER SISTERS
STILLBORN
STILLBORN
END OF THE 18TH DYNASTY
Tomb?
Nefertiti?
Kiya?
Ay?
MEMPHIS
AMARNA
EGYPT
NILE
GIZA
CAIRO
LUXOR
(THEBES)
J.

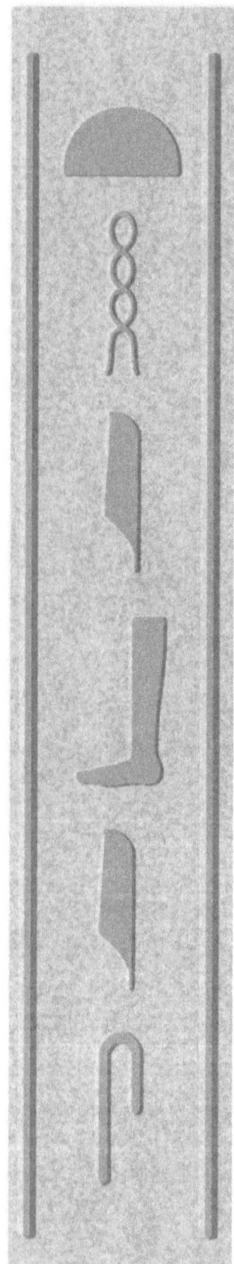

The University of Luxor
1818 Kornish Al Nile
Luxor City, Luxor, Egypt

Dear Ms. Sanura Taha,

Thank you for your interest in the UnderLine program at the University of Luxor's School of Archaeology. We would like to formally extend an invitation to join this excavation season's cohort.

We are excited to welcome you as a representative of Stanford University among a select group of students from institutions across the world for the opportunity to experience field excavation under the guidance of Dr. James Campbell of Oxford University.

Dr. Campbell is a world-renowned Egyptologist and pioneer in the use of X-ray fluorescence for artifact analysis. Students will spend eight weeks with Dr. Campbell and his team on-site in Luxor in collaboration with the Egyptian Ministry of Antiquites.

To retain your spot, please reply to this email no later than January 24th with an image of one form of government-issued identification (front and back) as an attachment.

Should you have any questions, feel free to email f_hadi@uofluxor.edu.eg. We look forward to hearing from you soon.

Regards,

Shareif Wahid
Admissions Director for UnderLine
The University of Luxor

Chapter 1

"Don't you think you should bring more clothes? You're going to be gone for two months!"

Mom's freakishly short arm was elbow-deep in a jumbo bag of "Feel the Heat" kettle-cooked barbecue chips while she leaned against my headboard.

"You know I don't like to check in luggage," I said, tossing my *Learn Arabic in 30 Days* handbook into my carry-on roller. They should really have called it *Learn Arabic or Go Blind Trying* because anyone who valued their sense of sight the least bit deserved a warning about the damaging effects of reading five hundred and forty-two pages printed in seven-point font.

Checking in luggage was always a hassle. The lines for the drop-off counters were especially excruciating when summer travelers flocked to the airports in droves in their shorts and flip flops. International travel was already a lengthy process, and the last thing that I wanted to do after nearly a day of traveling was stand at the luggage carousel and try to distinguish my suitcase from the sea of identical bags on display.

No. If I was flying all the way to Egypt, I didn't want to waste a single minute that could be better spent exploring my new surroundings.

"Still, you're going to be in the desert all day for eight weeks, sweating in the hot sun. You're surely going to need more than a couple of pairs of pajamas to change into at the end of the day, Kitty. Do they even have a washing machine at the hotel?"

Mom's chomping was growing louder by the minute with all the talking and open-mouthed chewing she was doing on my bed. She'd better pray I didn't find red seasoning dust on my sheets, or I'd be bunking with her tonight, and I knew how she hated my habit of watching Turkish dramas—subtitles on but the volume extra loud—late into the night on my iPad. My *oohs* and *aahs* complemented by tearful sniffles weren't exactly soothing to a bedmate at two in the morning.

"It's not a *hotel*," I corrected. "It's a *hostel*. And I'm sure I'll be okay. People go backpacking for like six months in Europe with two sets of clothes all the time."

I was certain that my five outfits, complete with breathable linen shirts, jeans, and flowy skirts, and two pairs of pajamas were quite enough for the trip. As far as underwear, I'd opted for my most comfortable, made of cotton. The desert sun was said to be unforgiving, and I didn't need to worry about getting a heat rash under my boobs, or God forbid, on my *cooch*.

"What if you go out somewhere nice like for dinner or something?" Mom countered as she stared into the chip bag. She had evidently blazed through the contents already and now resorted to tipping the bag into her open mouth to catch the crumbs.

"You better not get any crumbs on my bed," I scolded, imagining being poked by a million razor-sharp, well-seasoned potato shards. "And I'm going on a dig, not to party it up with Egypt's finest." In about forty-eight hours, my life would be devoted to the whims of Dr. Campbell, PhD, and his excavation team.

Mom abandoned the empty bag of chips and readjusted herself into a cross-legged position before dusting her hands off on her chinos with no regard for my warning or her clothes. For such a cute woman, she really operated more like a frat boy.

"I just want you to find time to enjoy yourself, too. You're flying all the way to your father's home country for the first time. This visit is more than just an internship. It's a chance to reconnect with your heritage." Her clear blue eyes shined glassy behind a film of wetness that threatened to puncture my chest.

I couldn't lie. When I had seen the announcement for the internship open to third-years in the Stanford Archaeology newsletter in my email, my heart had throbbed in my chest. It was an ache for something that I had never had before—a connection to my father's heritage.

I didn't remember much of Mohammed Taha, lovingly known to me as *Baba*. He'd passed away when I was only four years old. According to Mom, he had migrated from Egypt to California to study computer programming in college and had ended up meeting another aspiring programmer named Wendy, my mother, and falling in love. They had married after completing their bachelor's degrees and soon discovered they were expecting me.

Mom said that he'd been the one to pick my birth name, Sanura, which meant "kitten." I'd ended up going by Kitty early on because it was easier for Americans to pronounce.

I'd been nearly three years old when Baba had been diagnosed with a brain tumor. His health had declined rapidly soon after his diagnosis. Unfortunately for him, his own parents had passed away years prior, leaving him and his younger brother, Yusuf, to be raised by family. Yusuf had planned to visit us while my father was sick, but according to Mom, Baba hadn't wanted anyone to see him sick. The hair loss and constant nausea from chemotherapy and radiation and tumultuous seizures had been too much for Baba's pride to handle his baby brother seeing. Then, shortly after my fourth birthday, Baba had woken up one night vomiting uncontrollably, and Mom had rushed him to the ER. He'd never come back home.

Flash forward to now, I was a twenty-one-year-old half Egyptian, half American who had just learned enough Arabic per my degree requirement to carry on a conversation. At first glance, I looked Middle Eastern with my olive skin, large almond-shaped eyes, and long, thick, curly dark hair that reached just above my ass. And speaking of ass, that was definitely not something I'd gotten from my mom's delicate-featured side. My entire frame was thin with barely anything in the boob department, but my ass was round enough to warrant wearing one size larger than expected by the rest of my measurements.

My eyes were even dark brown like Baba's had been. Back in elementary school, I had always wished I could have pretty blue eyes and blonde hair like Mom so I could fit in better with the Ambers and Laurens, but that just wasn't in the A-T-C-G DNA base pair configuration that had been dealt to me.

Because of my looks, people expected me to speak Arabic fluently—especially other Middle Easterners I had met on the university campus—but if learning a foreign language hadn't been one of the requirements of my bachelor's, I probably would have struggled just to say "hello."

It wasn't my fault, though. I wanted to learn as much as I could about my culture, I just didn't have the tools to do so. And Mom tried to encourage my learning, but she was just as limited as I was in her knowledge. She didn't have any contact with Baba's family, and his brother Yusuf had never reached out again after Baba's death. So, when it had come time to choose what I wanted to study in college, Egyptology had been my first choice. It was a chance to learn the history of my people through the remains in the sand. To start from the beginning—the birth of their civilization.

"Just promise me you'll make some time to connect to your roots. This is a once-in-a-lifetime trip, and I want you to make the most out of it." Mom dabbed at her eyes, the guilt of not doing more to educate me about my history clearly eating at her.

But it wasn't her fault.

I lifted my palm in the air and placed my other hand over my heart, ready to dry her tears. "I swear to party like an Egyptian rock star in an effort to make this the most memorable trip of the century," I said solemnly, then bit my lip to contain the giggle threatening to break through.

A pillow immediately flew past my head. "That's not what I meant, smart ass!"

"So, is that a *no* to smoking hashish while I'm there?" I jabbed.

She flashed me her famous *don't-press-your-luck* look. "Sanura Taha, if I have to bail you out of an Egyptian jail, I'm never going to let you step foot out of this house again."

I rolled my eyes. "Boring!"

We both fell into fits of laughter.

Mom and I had a close relationship. It had always been just the two of us when I was growing up, so we had forged a bond that was more than just mother and daughter—we were best friends.

As a single mom working in Silicon Valley, Mom had often been burning the candle on both ends. She had started her career at a time when tech was solely a *bros' club*, so her managers had been less than understanding every time she had to rush home early when my school would call to say that I had a fever. But somehow, she had made it work, and for that, she was my role model.

Mom pulled out her phone and started playing on it as she spoke. *Candy Crush*, no doubt. "So, who is this professor that you'll be interning with?"

"Dr. Campbell. He's some famous Egyptologist from Oxford." I had heard his name often during my three years of undergrad and had even read some of his research papers for classes. His write-up on statistical models for establishing morphometric taxonomic identifications was breathtaking, if you could even use the term to describe a thirty-two-page paper complete with scatter-plot graphs and citations. In short, he was a genius in the field.

"Have you Googled him yet?" Mom asked.

"What? No. Why would I look him up?" He was probably just like every other legendary archaeologist: in his sixties and still a fan of tweed.

"Ummm, maybe to know who you're dealing with?! What if this guy is a hard-ass? Wouldn't you want to at least do your research before you meet him—to give you the upper hand?" That was Mom, always prepared for some bullshit to go down.

But I was the opposite. I was a child of my intuition and based major decisions on gut feelings. A scientist who listened to her heart over her brain—nothing sounded crazier. But it had worked for me ever since I'd begged Mom not to send me to Camp Culkin when I was eight. Apparently, the entire operation had had to be cancelled only three days in due to a widespread outbreak of Hepatitis A. Now, the real reason I hadn't wanted to go was so that I could spend the summer riding my new Barbie roadster bike, but I liked to think that my intuition had played a role in sparing my liver that summer.

"You know I don't believe in researching people before I meet them." I liked to give strangers the benefit of the doubt before meeting them so that we started off on a blank slate. Appearances were known to bias a person's impression before first words were ever spoken. Research would only lead to preconceived notions and false judgments about my preceptor or internship fellows, and I wanted to go into this experience with an open heart and an open mind. It could also be stressful knowing too much beforehand, and I didn't want that to ruin my excitement over the opportunity.

"Well, I do!" Mom tapped away at her phone. Her eyebrows nearly jumped off her forehead as she brought the screen almost flush with her face. "Holy shit!"

"What?" What could possibly be so surprising about Dr. Campbell? Archaeology was a male-dominated field, and most of the men looked similar across varying ethnicities: nonathletic build, middle-aged, and thinning hair.

I moved in closer to get a look at what Mom was ogling, curiosity getting the best of me. She pulled the phone away to her chest before I could peek. "I thought you didn't want to see?" She jutted her chin out at me, using my words against me. "What happened to giving people the benefit of the doubt?" Her lips rose into a smirk.

Straightening my spine, I pulled on the hem of my T-shirt, wishing it were my pride I were straightening out instead. "Fine. I don't want to see whatever it is you're looking at anyway." I was failing miserably to salvage my ego—I sounded like a bratty four-year-old swearing I'd hold my breath forever unless someone put a chilled juice box in my hand.

Mom snorted and shook her head like the image of me packing my suitcase for a long trip was too much for her to bear. "God, Kitty. I'm going to miss you so much."

The nagging anxiety that had been bubbling just under my overt excitement spilled over. I had never left Mom for longer than a week. What was I going to do without my best friend for two whole months?

Hot tears filled my eyes. "I'm going to miss you, too, Mom."

Chapter 2

"Please fasten your seatbelts. Cabin crew, please take your seats for landing."

The perky voice of the flight attendant enunciated through the intercom in perfect Arabic, drawing my attention away from the book on my tablet. I had gotten in some great reading time over the flight, with only about twenty percent of my romance novel left. The site that I watched my Turkish dramas on had been way too buggy on the plane's WiFi and I kept getting pop-ups with some woman with large boobs asking me if I wanted to play with her. Reading was the obvious second option to pass the time, and if you asked me, losing myself in a world where hope thrived and love conquered was the best distraction.

It reminded me of how I felt whenever I read about digs. Hope was what drove an archaeologist's work. Oftentimes, digs turned up nothing more than some broken pottery and animal bones, but the hope that something more would be discovered burned inside the chest of every scientist.

Dark waters stared back at me through the airplane window. Different hues of green mixed with tan completed the canvas—the canvas of my origins. A thrill of electricity buzzed through me, and my legs jittered restlessly, just itching to get me out of this plane so I could introduce myself to my motherland.

An elbow nudged at my arm on the rest between the seats.

"Good morning, sunshine!" I hummed to my neighbor.

Angela grunted her response as she wiped sleep from the corners of her eyes. Her noise-canceling headphones hung around her neck, so I knew she could hear me. The change in cabin pressure had probably disturbed her highness's beauty rest. I had started to worry she'd slipped into a coma or something since she had been passed out for the past nine hours. It had been a long flight after our layover in New York, but sleeping for that long uninterrupted on an airplane with numerous blaring announcements from the flight crew had to have been a world record for anyone.

With her golden-blonde hair trapped in a messy bun on top of her head, Angela chugged water clumsily from a plastic bottle like she was a boxer who'd just endured eight rounds before a knockout.

Her current disheveled state was in no way a true indicator of the Angela Bowman who graced the halls of Stanford. In fact, when she wasn't traveling, she looked like a living, breathing Barbie doll. It was certainly not the stereotypical persona of an archaeologist, but she was smart as fuck and deserved her spot in this internship.

Where I had small boobs and unruly hair, Angela had been blessed with ample curves and the smoothest hair I had ever seen. She turned heads wherever she went and was well aware of it, wearing only designer labels and accessories that were perfectly coordinated. That was why I had found it so amusing to see her show up to the airport before our flight in a velour tracksuit with a faded "Juicy" stamped on her ass. I hadn't even known people still owned such hideous athleisure wear. Was Juicy Couture even in business anymore?

My own college sweatshirt and jeans were comfortable yet unassuming enough for me.

Angela was a true Southern belle. Born and raised in Georgia, she hailed from a well-to-do family. Just going to get gas in her Porsche convertible qualified as a social event in her eyes; she wouldn't be caught dead in a tracksuit even at the local Chevron.

But she hated flying. She had taken so many white tablets at the start of each leg of our trip that I was pretty sure the associated drug-information pamphlets had warnings about dosing at the levels that were currently coursing through Angela's body. That would explain why she was no longer digging her nails into my arms like she had at take-off, and probably also why she had slept so long. Her stiletto nails proved to be long enough to have drawn blood from my tender skin, which had luckily scabbed over by now.

I was just thankful she had actually shown up because I had bet against myself that she would ditch the internship to spend her summer yachting off the coast of St. John with some hot deckhand named Ryan.

Reaching into the pocket on the back of the seat in front of me, I extracted a can of room-temperature Diet Coke and passed it to my left. "I saved this for you."

"God bless you," Angela croaked as she reached for the can.

I winced as she opened the tab—the click of her nails and dramatic *psssht* of the aluminum tab releasing gas rang louder than expected since I had popped my drums to accommodate the increase in air pressure. Still, I watched happily as my friend slurped down her can of caffeine, grateful that she'd opted out of first class to sit with me in coach.

Our bodies jolted forward as the plane made contact with the runway, eliciting claps around the cabin.

"Oh, thank God!" Angela proclaimed in her sweet Southern accent like she was front row in church on a Sunday as she signaled the sign of the cross on her chest. She wasn't particularly religious, but her Christian upbringing conveniently surfaced at times of duress.

I packed away my tablet into the cross-body bag in front of my feet. "You're feeling awfully spiritual today, aren't ya?"

"What time is it?" she asked, looking at the sun beating through the cabin window.

I checked the time on the media screen in front of me. "About three p.m. local time."

"Fuck. Why do I feel like it's four in the morning?" Angela groaned, rubbing her hands over her face.

"It's probably because of all the Xanax you took, and the time difference—but more so the pills."

"Bitch, you're lucky I took that many, else you would have had to peel me off the emergency exit."

"Nah, I would have just pretended not to know you," I teased.

The plane rolled forward, finally stopping at the gate. The *bing* on the sound system was a welcome relief. I immediately stood up, even though our row was toward the back and it would be a while before we deplaned. The rush of blood to my numb legs felt foreign after sitting for so long.

Slowly, the line ahead of us filed out of the plane. I kept busy on my phone catching up on my missed messages and updating my location on social media, thanks to my international plan. A gentle shove to the shoulder from Angela signaled I was holding up the line, so I moved into the aisle with my shoulder bag, ready to grab my roller bag from the overhead compartment.

"What's wrong?" Angela asked with her Louis Vuitton roller bag next to her, busy drawing the handle up.

My eyes flashed from compartment to compartment, unable to locate my black bag with the polka dot ribbon tied to the handle. "My bag's not here."

"What do you mean, it's not here? Where did you put it?"

I pointed to the now empty compartment as the line of passengers anxious to deboard murmured behind us.

"Damn. Someone must have taken off with your bag?"

"What am I going to do? I didn't bring any checked luggage." How was I going to manage two months in a foreign country without any of my clothes or toiletries? The cross-body bag that I did have was only big enough to carry my tablet, cellphone, and wallet and I'd had to stuff my laptop into my bigger carry-on bag. I needed that laptop if I were going to do any sort of research during this internship.

"Don't worry about that. You can wear my clothes until your bag shows up, but you should probably report it to the flight attendant."

I rushed to the front of the cabin, where three of the hostesses who'd served our flight were smiling their farewells through perfectly glossed lips.

In my sub-par Arabic, I explained that my luggage was missing.

My grammar must have been shaky because one of the women opted to continue the conversation in English. "Miss, if you believe your baggage was stolen, you will need to file a complaint at baggage claim. If by chance the bag is found, then they can contact you."

"What am I supposed to do without my bag?! I'm here for two months on an excavation project! What will I wear? What if my mentor assigns an impromptu project? How will I look up the mummification procedure of the eighteenth dynasty?!" The words flew out a mile a minute, leaving the English-speaking attendant slightly dazed, which only wove me deeper into the web of frustration that I had spun.

"I'm sorry that I cannot help you any further." Her lips fixed into a stern smile as she eyed the line of people behind me, signaling that my time on the plane had officially expired.

"Come on, Kitty." Angela wrapped her hand around my wrist and led me along. "We'll talk to the agent at baggage claim and see what they can do. Hopefully, someone just took it by accident and they'll return it."

I hoped she was right, because if it had been stolen, then I'd be placing an ancient Egyptian–style curse on the *klepto* who had my bag. Although, I'd need my laptop to Google ancient Egyptian curses first. *Fucking irony.*

The line to speak to a baggage agent was insanely long, so I told Angela to go ahead and collect her luggage from the carousel while I waited. One hour and forty minutes later, and I still felt as hopeless as I had when I'd first discovered my bag was gone. All that time spent just to get to the counter to give my name, cell number, and the address of the hostel that the university had set up for us. The old "don't call us, we'll call you," *Egyptian edition.*

Tired and empty-handed, I found Angela waiting for me near the exit doors.

"No luck with the bag?"

My shoulders slumped even lower. "They said they'll call me, but who knows if that'll even happen."

Angela sighed. "I'm just glad that I packed multiple bags for this very reason." I knew my lost luggage was just a convenient justification for over-packing, but I decided to humor her this time for the sake of the extra outfits I could borrow.

Despite the rough start, I wasn't going to let this get me down. My journey had yet to begin, and I wasn't going to waste the beginning of it stressing over something I couldn't control like stolen luggage. Straightening my spine and lifting my chin, I grabbed one of Angela's bags. "Come on, let's go find our shuttle outside."

Chapter 3

The drive to the hostel was only about twenty minutes, most of it spent on a highway that was packed to capacity with vehicles. As soon as we exited, the roads narrowed significantly. We'd entered a densely packed region of buildings, all stone-colored and tightly packed together. Thankfully, the tiny car that the internship program had arranged to have pick us up could fit all of Angela's bags, because I didn't know how we'd have fit on the slender street if we'd had to take an SUV.

The pair of clear stringed beads that adorned the rearview mirror swayed abruptly, casting specks of prism light around as the car jerked to a stop.

"Oh, thank Jesus!" Angela exclaimed, bolting out of the car. "I'm dying in this sauna. It's too damn hot!"

I rolled my eyes at her ever-present dramatic flair and followed her outside. "How on earth did you decide on becoming an archaeologist?" It wasn't a glamorous job. Most countries that held internships during dig seasons had hot weather and required teams to be out in the sun from sunrise to sunset.

But I had to agree with her, *it was too damn hot*. Even with my sweatshirt tied around my waist and my hair up in a messy bun at the top of my head, I was dripping with sweat.

Angela shrugged as she tipped the driver for unloading her bags. "I like vintage things."

Her eyes settled on the weathered, beige-colored building in front of us. A flashy red sign that read "Luxor Hostel" was proudly displayed over the front door. Dull brown paint outlined the glass entrance, with dark wood shutters hanging alongside the windows.

A look of horror washed over her face. "What kind of hotel is this?"

"A vintage one," I teased, smirking as I wheeled one of her bags through the doors. I supposed she had missed the memo on our assigned accommodations.

The interior was much more bright and cheerful than the exterior. Greens, yellows, and reds were splashed all over the walls as paint and tiles. The floor resembled something I had seen once in a 1920s coffee-table book of Egyptian lodgings. The whole vibe made me feel giddy to explore the country.

My excitement, however, was in stark contrast to Angela's shock. Her eyes bounced from the check-in desk to the communal dining table right next to it, covered in a light blue vinyl tablecloth.

I had never stayed in a hostel before, but based on stories I had heard from friends who frequented them, I'd expected this kind of atmosphere. My friends swore that this was the best way to travel on a budget, and it seemed like the internship program agreed.

"I am *not* staying here," Angela muttered under her breath so the gentleman at the front desk couldn't hear.

"Don't be ridiculous! This place is so charming!" I spun around in place, just noticing the mosaic tiles on the ceiling for the first time as my sweatshirt tails danced around my waist. After a gleeful three-sixty, I approached the counter.

"Welcome to Luxor Hostel. Checking in?" the man asked in heavily accented English. He seemed to be a little older than us, maybe by a year or two, with dark hair and a short, scruffy beard.

"Yes, we're here for the archaeology intern program. My name is Kitty. . .um, Sanura Taha, and this is my friend Angela Bowman." I signaled to my friend over my shoulder and saw she still looked like she was ready to hightail it out the door at any moment.

Angela gave a weak wave.

"*Egyptian?*" the man asked in Arabic with interest. My name coupled with my thick curls spilling out of my poorly composed bun was probably the giveaway.

"*Half. My father was born here,*" I answered back in Arabic.

That earned me a nod with a warmer smile. "*Welcome home.*"

It was like, in that moment, I wasn't just a tourist visiting a foreign land, even though I should have felt that way. This stranger felt some sort of camaraderie with me based on a shared heritage. I hadn't expected that to happen here...I had expected to feel more like an outsider since I'd been born in America and spoke only the Arabic that I had learned from my bachelor's program.

The man typed something into the desktop in front of him. I focused on the array of signs behind him as the keys clicked, all written in English for out-of-town travelers, no doubt: "Free Wi-Fi"; "No Alcohol on Premises"; "No Noise from Sunset to Sunrise."

"You will be in room five at the top of the stairs on the left," he replied in English this time as he eyed Angela behind me. He passed me a set of keys for each of us. "We serve three meals a day for the entire hostel, but you are free to use the private kitchen in the back if you would like meals in between with your own foods from the market."

"What? No room service?" Angela huffed out in disbelief.

"Thank you." I smiled earnestly, anxious to shove Angela in our room so she'd quit embarrassing herself.

"We have to take the stairs?" Angela had her hands on her hips, looking at me as if I'd had something to do with the decision not to install an elevator.

"Oh, come on, diva! Your ass should be so tight from all those kickboxing classes," I teased, careful to keep my voice low enough so the receptionist wouldn't overhear my use of the word *ass*. I wasn't sure how conservative he was, though he had probably seen a lot running a hostel.

I grabbed two of Angela's bags and rolled them toward the stairs. Luckily, there weren't too many steps, but the stairway was narrow, so I had to stand at the top of each step and pull the bigger suitcase up like my life depended on it.

Winded and muscles shaking, we made it to the top.

"Room five," I read off the door. "This is it." I slipped the key into the lock of the wobbly knob and the door pushed open.

Angela tipped her chin up to the sky and scrunched her eyes shut. "Oh, sweet Jesus. Why is this happening to me?"

"Leave Jesus alone. He's busy staving off famine. It's not that bad! Look, we have air-conditioning." My eyes bounced around the quaint room, from the large AC unit overhead to the two twin-sized beds with white sheets and flannel blankets on top. Plain white walls encased the room and the only access to the outside was a small window between the beds. Sure, the décor was lacking, but archaeologist lodgings weren't extravagant. Grants awarded for digs were usually slim and researchers didn't want to waste all of the funds granted on five-star hotels and gourmet meals. The digs were for such a short amount of time, and we were expected to tough it out.

Angela plopped onto the bed, the springs creaking under her back. "I can't believe that I could have been on a yacht in the Caribbean right now with a cocktail in my hand."

I lay down next to her, ignoring the stiffness of the mattress under me. "But then you'd be missing out on '*the adventure of a lifetime*,'" I sang, quoting an excerpt from the description section of the internship listing.

She turned her head to me. "How the fuck are you so insanely optimistic, yet we're such good friends?" For a girl who called on Jesus as much as she did, she sure had the mouth of a sailor. A good *Christian* sailor.

I shrugged. "Because I'm just so loveable. Now, give me some of your clothes so I can go take a shower and wash off the airplane stink."

I was dead tired after the day we'd had and I needed enough rest to survive the first day of our internship tomorrow. We had to be up at 4 a.m., and I just hoped our mentor was the high point of this experience, because Lord knew that Angela's patience would be non-existent when she had to wake up that early.

Chapter 4

The common area was bustling with the chatter of interns, a stark contrast to when we had arrived at check-in yesterday. The hostel was also open to other travelers, but if there were any, none seemed to be awake at this hour of the morning.

Our internship team was only five bodies large, but the excitement of the day ahead rippled through each of us—all, except Angela.

"Mornin', sunshine," I chirped as I took a sip of the strong coffee set before me.

It was a little after four in the morning and we had to leave on the shuttle in about fifteen minutes.

Angela and I had been dead tired after unpacking and getting cleaned up, so we had both decided to skip dinner and sleep off the jet lag instead. I had set the alarm on my phone to wake up on time, but we'd had an unexpected wakeup call echoing through the streets instead. I was aware that the call to prayer sounded five times per day in Arab countries, but I hadn't realized it would start as early as three in the morning. Imagine our surprise when a male voice had rang through the silence of the early morning hours. I had nearly fallen out of my bed startled, but Sleeping Beauty over here had rolled over and covered her head with a pillow and gone back to sleep.

Angela grunted her greeting before collapsing into the chair across from me. She might be a crank, but she looked ready to tackle her first day on a dig, appropriate in her Stanford burnout T-shirt and khaki pants.

"By the way, thanks for these awesome clothes." I motioned to the outfit she had laid out for me to borrow the night before.

She gulped her coffee unceremoniously. "What are you griping about? You look great. You could use more clothes to show off your curves."

"My wardrobe is just fine, thank you very much. We were told to dress conservatively, not like we're heading out to the club in the early 2000s!"

"Hey, I resent that. I just bought that outfit three weeks ago. The sales lady said bodycon is making a comeback. Get with it or get out." She stuffed her mouth with the breakfast in front of her: salted fava beans with hard-boiled eggs and pita.

The internship coordinator had sent us an email with customs to be mindful of when we traveled to Egypt. It explained specifically that conservative wear was required. We were instructed to be sure that our knees and shoulders were covered in public and that our clothes were not to fit too tightly against our bodies. I was certain that the short-sleeve, neon-pink bodycon top, which I suspected Angela had intended as a dress, and skinny jeans clearly violated the "tightness" rule. Luckily, my tits were smaller than Angela's, which afforded me some extra room in the top. But I could barely pull the jeans over my hips, let alone zip them. Thank God for the hair-tie hack I'd learned on TikTok to keep them buttoned! I was also lucky that Angela had packed some neck scarves to double as head scarves, which the coordinator had recommended we bring in case we wanted to visit any mosques during our stay. I was using the white scarf she'd loaned me as a shawl to cover most of my top from view.

I reminded myself to call the airlines later to see if they had located my bag. Something told me I wouldn't survive the embarrassment of Angela's wardrobe for much longer.

Suddenly, a devastatingly handsome guy sat down next to Angela. "Hey, I'm Felipe. Are you two ladies the Stanford participants?" His thick Spanish accent was warm and inviting. His boyish smile coupled with the dark hair on top of his head and stubble on his square jaw made him look like one of those cute professional soccer players.

The tiredness in Angela's eyes instantly vanished as the setting on her make-believe battery pack switched to "flirt mode." She jutted her boobs out in Felipe's direction, the school logo on her shirt standing at full attention. "Were we that obvious?" The playful grin on her lips was like sugar mixed with honey—way too *extra*.

Not as obvious as you undressing poor Felipe with your eyes.

His smile shone bright while he politely avoided the tits in his face as best he could.

"You must be from the University of Madrid. I'm Kitty." I extended my hand over the table.

He took it, giving it a gentle squeeze—nothing awkward, just friendly. The internship program had sent out an email letting us know which universities had been selected to participate this year, and judging from his accent, he was the selection from Spain.

"And I'm Angela." She grabbed his hand before the guy even had a chance to offer it.

Angela's favorite hobby was men. Back in California, she had her pick of the lot, rarely ever seeing the same one twice. I admired her assertiveness— to go out there and take what she wanted. I wished I was just as bold. I'd had boyfriends in the past, but I could count them on the fingers of one hand. My dating life had hit a stale point lately, and Angela was putting me to shame by snagging the best-looking guy on our team.

"Are you two excited for today?" Felipe asked. "This is the first dig I've ever participated in."

"Same for the both of us. I don't know what to expect," I replied. I had only read about excavations in research papers and seen them in documentaries, so the thrill of participating in a live one was something I still couldn't quite believe.

"I just can't wait to get dirty, you know?" Angela's lips tipped up into a sly grin aimed straight for her Spanish crush.

Nervously eyeing her as if she were a hungry python in the hands of a zookeeper in a petting exhibit, Felipe continued, "It should be a lot of fun, even though I heard that Dr. Campbell can be rather *difficult*."

"Ugh, don't tell me he's a hard-ass," Angela groaned. "It's bad enough we need to be up at the crack of dawn; now I need to worry about some man who has small-dick syndrome or something getting on my case." Her Southern accent was always stronger when she was irritated.

"It's true," the guy sitting to my left added. "Hi, I'm Sean." His British accent meant that he was most likely the team member from Cambridge. He seemed to be a few years older than us, with a dark head of hair just like Felipe, but where Felipe had a scruffier appearance, Sean was well groomed and looked like he should have been teaching a class himself with his white linen shirt and dark blue jeans.

I introduced both of us this time around. "I'm Kitty, and this is Angela."

"It's a pleasure," he replied with a courteous smile only half as big as Felipe's was.

"Do you know Dr. Campbell?" Angela asked, redirecting the conversation back to the topic of our mentor.

"I don't. But my friend goes to Oxford and took one of his classes. She said he was the hardest grader she'd ever had. Just barely passed his final."

"Shit . . ." I frowned. I hadn't thought that our mentor would be the professor from hell. All the hope and excitement I'd had oozed away. I wasn't a worrier by nature, but a foreign feeling slowly crept into my chest—*anxiety*.

"*Difficult* isn't necessarily a bad thing. Maybe he just wants us to learn as much as possible," a raven-haired woman with delicate features said, interjecting. Her petite frame was on display as she leaned over the table, resting her hand on the surface as she spoke to us. Her accent was distinctly Italian, making her the fifth and final member of our team from the University of Rome.

"And who are you?" Angela asked pointedly, not liking that Hermione Granger had invited herself into our conversation.

"Isa-bel-la." Even the way she said her name, enunciating each syllable so that we would remember it, came off as pretentious. I had the sneaking suspicion that she was going to ask Dr. Campbell to add a research assignment to our program before the sun set today.

"I don't know about you, but I like to learn without a micromanaging dictator hovering over me," Felipe joked. This earned a disapproving scowl from Isabella.

"Forgive me for being so forward, but if I had to fly all the way here, then I'd want to get the most out of this experience," she snapped, glowering at him.

The group stared at her. We all wanted to get the most out of this trip, but shit, not all on the first day!

Sean's voice broke the tension. "Well, I think we should head out so we're not late."

Everyone agreed and grabbed their dishes to hand them back to the cook. The table looked just as tidy as it had been before we woke up for breakfast.

"Everyone got their sacks?" Sean asked.

I looked around at my teammates, all of whom—especially overachiever Isabella—had backpacks filled with notebooks, pens, and water bottles slung over their shoulders. Everyone except me.

I was disappointingly unprepared for the most important experience of my college career.

Dear God, please help me to get through this day unscathed!

Chapter 5

The desert.

Miles and miles of powdery sand, littered with jagged rocks. My breath hitched in my chest at the sight of pale gold dunes as I peered out the window.

All the images I had seen in textbooks and documentaries simply hadn't done the sight before me justice. This land held thousands of years of history under it, just waiting for someone to listen closely for the secrets it contained.

The chills running down my spine were inexplicable, but they reminded me this was my passion. In this moment, I knew the work that I was about to do here was my calling. I was certain of it.

According to the information we'd received about the internship, this dig was a continuation of one from last season. Dr. Campbell's team had unearthed a temple dating back to the eighteenth dynasty, specifically from the era of noteworthy names like Akhenaten, Nefertiti, and the all-famous King Tut. It had been constructed sometime after the death of Pharaoh Akhenaten, the king who'd attempted to make Egypt a monotheistic country. During his reign, he had even changed the capital from Thebes to Amarna, which was four hours north of where we were. After his death, his only son and predecessor, Tutankhamun removed his royal court from Amarna and restored the practice of polytheism to the country. In an effort to revolt against the monotheistic rule that had once governed them, ancient Egyptians had desecrated many of the monuments devoted to Akhenaten and subsequently Tutankhamen, even though King Tut had reversed many of his father's ordinances.

The temple that Dr. Campbell's team had unearthed last year was believed to have been built sometime soon after Tutankhamen's reign. The question was: who built it, and why?

A fog of hot dust hit my face as the car door opened, but I was eager to exit the cramped space and jumped without hesitation. Stretching my legs after the forty-minute drive felt glorious. The five of us had squished into the four available seats in the beat-up Land Cruiser. And I had somehow been volunteered as the one who had to lean forward all bunched up like a fetus.

The morning sunlight, though it wasn't at its most severe yet, still had the power to pierce my corneas. I squinted through tears, wishing I had my sunglasses.

My ankles rolled as I stepped past the bank of larger rocks and my shoes filled with sand. Unfortunately, all I had in the way of footwear were the ballet flats I had worn on the plane, since my hiking boots, and sadly missed sunglasses, were somewhere in the abyss with all the other lost luggage in the universe, probably next to that place where socks go missing from the dryer.

"This is amazing!" I felt the earth shift beside my feet and glanced over to see Felipe taking in the surroundings through aviator shades while I used my hand to shield the sun from my frame of view.

I looked to where he was focused and saw a simple stone structure. Mudbricks laid atop one another formed a simple cube-shaped building with a very unassuming entrance that seemed too narrow for a human to enter. The appearance was sloppily constructed, something passersby would overlook if they saw it through their windshield. For a temple from the time of pharaohs, it was rather underwhelming and small, about the size of a cheap studio apartment. The desert around it seemed much more magnificent in comparison.

Just off to the side of the stone structure was a large white tent with men busy organizing tools and equipment that would be needed for today's work. Two figures stood huddled close in conversation in front of the team. One was short and stocky with a rounded middle section that filled out his denim shirt and matching jeans. His mostly bald head was brown just like the rest of his skin with an outline of gray hair around the edge.

The other man had a frame opposite his comrade's. He was tall and looked to be in excellent shape, judging from how his white shirt molded to his muscles. Dark blue jeans hung low on his hips. He was younger than the other man, maybe somewhere in his late thirties or early forties, just based on his full head of hair. Though sunglasses shielded his expression as he spoke to the shorter man, he appeared to be engaged in a tense conversation which resulted in his spine standing rigid like a rod.

The shorter man looked away having noticed our arrival. He quickly wiped his shiny head with a handkerchief before pocketing it and plopping on a wide-brimmed straw hat. His feet crunched on small rocks as he approached us. I took him for our mentor, going by his forwardness and assumed years of experience in the field.

"Welcome. Welcome." He spoke to us in English, his voice high-pitched and speech hurried. "I am Mohammed Tasvir, the foreman for this excavation, but you may call me Mo."

Foreman? I looked around the group to see if anyone else seemed as baffled as I was, but they all remained unaffected, like they had already known who the man was. *Fuck you, Google.*

My eyes shot to the looming figure next to Mo, who was now staring at us through the dark lenses of his shades.

Damn.

Mo continued speaking at a quick pace. "I hope you are ready to work because we have a lot to accomplish today. Now, I will pass the floor to your mentor for the next eight weeks." He lifted his hand high to place it on Mr. Serious's shoulder.

The man removed his glasses, revealing deep blue eyes, like the lapis lazuli that decorated the ancient death masks of the pharaohs. Sandy-blond hair streaked with highlights from sun exposure glistened in the sunlight.

Fuck me. Not literally. Well, maybe. Who could think straight with *that* standing in front of them?

And what kind of archaeological expert was so damn young and hot? Surely, there were rules about the limit of attractiveness for professors, since nearly all the ones I had seen were over the age of fifty and didn't boast movie-star good looks.

My eyes darted around the group, but everyone just continued standing at attention as if a dirty-blond Brendan Fraser from his *Mummy* days hadn't just waltzed into our lives. The only other person who seemed somewhat affected was Angela, who was focusing on pouting her glossed lips, pulling her shoulders back, and tilting her hips forward—her mating dance, if you will.

Those vibrant eyes, framed by tiny wrinkles at the corners, waded through our group, taking in each of our faces as if committing it to memory.

"As you've guessed, I'm James Campbell," he began, his thick voice laden with a British accent that twisted my insides.

Why the fuck hadn't I researched the man before coming here? Instead, I'd wanted to go into this blind like some "feel the vibe" hippie. If I'd only listened to my mother, I wouldn't be standing here gawking at my dreamy mentor like a loser. *So professional, Kitty.*

"You were selected from a long list of outstanding applicants."

Isabella's spine straightened an inch taller as she gleamed with pride.

Dr. Campbell continued, "This means that I have the highest expectations for each of you. The next few weeks are not going to be easy or glamorous." His stern tone commanded the attention of anyone within earshot. Even Mo was hanging on his every word. "This isn't a vacation, so if you came here expecting to smoke water pipe under a palm tree, then I suggest you call your mother and have her book you a one-way ticket home."

He crossed his arms over his chest, the tight cords in his tanned forearms flexing with the movement. None of us escaped his scrutinizing gaze as he slowly paced in front of us. "I expect professionalism from each of you. I won't tolerate lateness, nor will I tolerate unpreparedness."

He directed his attention toward Angela, who flashed him her most sultry smile—the one where one side of her mouth rose higher than the other. I had seen many a grown man fall victim to that smile, and let me tell you, ten out of ten red-blooded men took the bait.

Dr. Campbell was the exception. None of his body parts twitched, nor did the rise and fall of his broad chest falter. Instead, he moved onto Felipe, completely unamused.

"I will be on-site every day. You will have Fridays and Saturdays off, but all other days, you belong to me."

Felipe's throat worked as he swallowed nervously under the weight of Dr. Campbell's glare.

"Following my rules should be simple, especially since I have been so nice as to outline each of them to you."

God, help me—I was next.

My breath quickened and my fingers and toes tingled as I waited for my turn in this makeshift soldier lineup.

Dr. Campbell centered himself in front of me and continued speaking. "And I don't take too kindly to being disobeyed." His severe gaze held mine. "So don't tempt me," he added, enunciating the word "tempt" excruciatingly slowly, the severity of his Ts nicking my ears. Heat rushed to my already overheated cheeks. *Could he see them reddening?*

His chiseled jaw coupled with his full lips made him a difficult sight to avoid. I must have been violating all sorts of internship policies by paying too much attention to his facial anatomy.

Yet his eyes...they were hypnotizing, like staring into the sun for too long.

I was the first to break eye contact, unable to bear their intensity any longer. But he remained in place. I could feel the heat of his glare on my chest, as he studied my obnoxiously pink shirt.

After what seemed like years, he moved onto Sean. "Are there any questions?"

Isabella raised her hand. *Of course, she couldn't stay quiet.*

Dr. Campbell stepped in front of her. "Introduce yourself," he ordered.

"Isabella Bianchi from The University of *Roma*," she answered, matching his military-like tone. While the rest of us seemed to be scared shitless by *Dr. Devil,* Isabella seemed to appreciate his attitude.

"What is your question, Isabella?"

"Will we have the opportunity to complete research projects of our own in addition to the research performed during the excavation?"

This bitch was just asking to be popped in the face. Day one and she's asking for more work?! *Unbelievable.* I rolled my eyes with an exaggerated attitude, hoping she'd see.

"Did you want to add anything to her question?" Dr. Campbell barked at me, catching the tail end of my exasperation.

"Me?" I pointed at my own chest, startled. His expression remained hard. "Um, I...um. No." I shook my head profusely.

His eyes stayed glued to me as he addressed Isabella and her question. "That will not be necessary. I anticipate that you'll find yourselves to be too occupied with the work that we have to do here to conduct your own assignments.

"And you," he directed at me. "What is your name?"

Again, everything came out as a stutter. "I...um...me? I'm...um...Kitty Taha."

Mo produced a wad of paper from his pocket and unfolded it. His thick, white eyebrows pinched as he examined the contents. "There is no Kitty Taha on the list!" he exclaimed, shaking the paper at me.

"Oh, maybe it's under my real first name, Sanura?" I had used my legal name for my application.

Mo nodded in acceptance. "You're Egyptian?" His voice hitched with excitement.

Dr. Campbell's eyes had never strayed from me, so I wasn't sure who to address. My focus bounced between the two men. "Yes, on my father's side," I said, opting for the short-and-sweet answer. I didn't want to divulge my entire diary's worth of history about my father's death and my quest to connect with my heritage when I was already making such a stellar first impression.

"Why do you go by Kitty?" Dr. Campbell's voice hung heavy in the air between us.

"It's, um...a pet name," I squeaked.

"A pet name for the kitten?" he asked.

I stared at him in confusion, heart hammering. *Surely, he didn't mean—*

"*Sanura* means 'kitten,' does it not?" His expression was flat.

"Oh, right." For a second, I'd thought he was referring to *something else*, not the meaning of my name.

With a hike of his brow, Dr. Campbell hesitated a moment longer before stalking back toward the tent, leaving us to gawk at him through the dust left in his wake.

The group looked at each other, unsure of what to do next, until Isabella suddenly jutted forward, nearly breaking out into a run to catch up to Dr. Campbell. Without a better idea, we followed her lead.

Dr. Campbell didn't hesitate to get down to business and began spewing out information at warp speed. The rest of the group fished out their notebooks from their backpacks and started scribbling notes furiously as he spoke. I was once again empty-handed and tried my hardest to commit everything to memory.

"This temple was built sometime after the death of Tutankhamen in 1324 BC. We deduced this from radio-carbon dating analysis performed on bones we believe belonged to animals that were most likely used as offerings for worship."

"What kinds of animals?" Isabella asked as she jotted words furiously into her leather-bound notebook while walking.

"Cats," he answered bluntly.

Cats had been considered sacred by the ancient Egyptians, so it was certainly fitting that the remains were feline.

A pet name for the kitten?

Goosebumps broke out along the back of my neck at the memory of his words. Shaking them off as quickly as they had appeared in my head, I listened more intently.

"Was it built in honor of Tutankhamen?" Sean asked.

"It would seem so, based on the cartouche inside and the drawings on the wall," Dr. Campbell continued. A cartouche was an oval design with the name of a royal in hieroglyphs. "It would seem that it was built with the intention of worshipping Tutankhamen."

"Didn't he have other temples constructed during his life? What's so special about this one?" Angela asked. Strangers might have mistaken her as superficial, but she was one smart cookie when it came to the field.

"That's a great question," Dr. Campbell added. "He did, especially his mortuary temple that would have been used to worship him after his death—which has yet to be discovered."

"This is far too small to be a mortuary temple." Isabella turned her nose up in the air as if she were the famed Egyptologist in the group and not Dr. Campbell.

He didn't seem to take any offense at her tone. "It would seem so."

"According to my research, there aren't any temples recorded to have been constructed in this area. Is that true?" Felipe asked.

"That's correct," Dr. Campbell said. "None exist in this area for any other pharaohs, either."

It was strange for a temple devoted to a pharaoh to be so humble and out in the middle of nowhere. "So, then who built it?" I asked.

Dr. Campbell stopped in his tracks, causing his tail of students to halt abruptly as well.

He turned around to face me. His eyes scanned my chest. "Why aren't you taking notes?"

"My luggage was stolen on the flight." My voice shook as I spoke. The man was intimidating, and I wasn't used to being this meek in the presence of anyone. I was starting to annoy myself with how fragile I sounded.

"What does that have to do with anything?" he quipped impatiently. Everyone stared, waiting for my response.

"It's just that all of my research material and notebooks were in my bag, too."

"And your shoes?" He eyed my black ballet flats, a slightly amused smile hitching up one corner of his mouth.

I threw my hands in the air to lighten the mood. "Airlines! They'd lose passengers if they weren't strapped to the seats." The laugh that came out of my throat sounded about two octaves higher than my already high-pitched voice.

Felipe suppressed a chuckle from behind his hand, and Angela smacked his shoulder to remind him to stay in check. And all Dr. Campbell did was grumble something under his breath that I couldn't make out, before marching toward the tent.

I trudged behind, Angela walking next to me. "He hates me. Five minutes into this internship, and my mentor thinks I'm dense as a doorstop."

"Oh, stop! He doesn't think that. You just got off to a bad start," she said, squeezing my arm gently. "It'll get better."

I hoped to God she was right.

Chapter 6

Note to self: Angela Bowman was a liar and her previously occupied seat as "best college friend who happened to always score free drinks" was now available to the highest bidder.

Things hadn't improved on the site. Dr. Campbell's annoyance had become *more* evident, and it was only the second day. The rest of the group wasn't spared from his snappy nature, but I seemed to bear the brunt of it.

Anytime I hesitated for more than three seconds before answering one of his pop quiz questions, he'd bark at me for wasting his time. If I took too long grabbing him a tool that he was too lazy to get on his own, he'd mutter far too loudly that I was holding him back from his schedule. The man was incorrigible.

The only bright light of this internship was the generosity of my team members, *sans* Isabella, of course. Felipe had been kind enough to loan me an extra notebook and pen and Sean had gifted me a reusable canvas bag with "Waterstones" printed in large font over a sketch of books sitting on shelves.

As far as clothes were concerned, Angela had done only a slightly better job at *styling* me today. The tan Banana Republic jumpsuit with cuffed sleeves and legs was less body-hugging than the previous day's outfit, but I looked like a zookeeper doing lunch at the café on the third floor of a Nordstrom department store. At least my nipples weren't ready to rip through fabric anymore.

"Sanura, what is taking so long?" The sharp edge in Dr. Campbell's voice had the uncanny ability to my eye twitch.

While my team members and Dr. Campbell's workers were preoccupied digging and clearing away debris from around the temple foundation, he had sent me on a hunt for specimen bags to secure some pottery fragments.

I couldn't find them.

Sweat slicked my skin in the suffocating heat. Even though I was shielded from the hot afternoon sun under the tent, its presence was inescapable under shelter. I had never sweat so much underneath my boobs in my life, and the synthetic material of Angela's jumpsuit wasn't helping one bit. What I wouldn't give to undo one, or four, of the gold buttons down my chest and air out like a thirsty spring-breaker in a bikini. I was sure that view would give a few of the older workers a stroke right on the spot.

With my unruly hair already in a topknot on my head, I fanned the back of my neck with my hand as my eyes scanned the area again, searching for the elusive clear plastic bags.

"*Check in there.*"

I looked up to find one of the workers, Abdul, nod toward a utility carrier on wheels. It was overflowing with brushes, mattocks for digging, rope, and trowels. I had already done a quick check of the contents and hadn't found what I was looking for.

"*I already checked,*" I replied to Abdul in Arabic.

He was dressed in a white floor-length tunic with long sleeves, and I wondered how he could stand to be so covered up when it was sweltering out here.

Instead of being frustrated with me like Dr. Campbell always seemed to be, Abdul offered me a genial smile and came over to the carrier. He fished through it again.

"*There they are!*" I exclaimed as relief washed over me. I could have kissed Abdul, but instead, I offered him an appreciative, "*Shukran,*" which meant "thank you."

Abdul nodded his acceptance.

But that voice roared through my ears again. "Sanuraaa!"

It was funny how my own name could grate my ears, but it seemed anything in the deep baritone of his voice could make the hairs on the back of my neck stand on end.

My feet scurried in the direction of a visibly fuming Dr. Campbell with his fists testily perched on his hips. The uneven rubble coupled with the unsteady sand had my steps twisting and turning in the clumsiest of ways. Suddenly, I lost my footing on a loose rock and jolted backward, sending clear bags soaring into the sky. Air rushed out of my lungs in a shrill screech as my ass slammed painfully onto the ground and my legs sprawled out in front of me.

My ankle! It throbbed murderously as I clutched my shin too scared to touch the injury.

"Kitty!" Angela called out as she ran to me. "Oh, my God! Are you okay?"

Within seconds, I was surrounded by the entire work team, all murmuring in various languages as they huddled over me. I wished some strategically positioned quicksand would magically appear and swallow me into the earth so I wouldn't die of humiliation in front of everyone.

The crowd parted to let Dr. Campbell through. Without hesitating, he knelt, quickly taking in the tears that had fallen down my face.

My shoe had flown off during the whole debacle, so Dr. Campbell directed his attention to my bare foot. He hastily rolled up the leg of my jumpsuit to just below my knee. His hands were about to land on my skin when I pushed them away.

"I'm fine," I managed to lie through the pain. I knew I needed medical attention, but it was too strange having my mentor fuss over me like an invalid.

"You're crying, Sanura. This isn't the time to play shy," he growled.

Mortified, I swiped at the tears on my face but held my tongue as he examined my ankle.

Calloused hands skimmed my skin. Years of working on sites in arid climates were probably the cause of the roughness of his fingers. He might have been a jerk, but his hands were proof that he didn't shy away from manual labor.

I watched his brows furrow as he pressed his fingers around my foot, his touch surprisingly gentle for a man so focused on the task at hand. His hand moved higher along my shin, causing an involuntary outbreak of goosebumps along my leg.

"Does this hurt?" Dr. Campbell applied slight pressure.

I shook my head.

He worked around the area, pressing on various points and asking me if I felt any discomfort. Nothing hurt unbearably but my toes curled from the massaging sensation. To be honest, it felt good. My legs had been sore from walking around in unsupportive ballet flats, and my shins felt achy. I wouldn't have been surprised if I had developed shin splints in addition to whatever had happened to my ankle.

Before I could help it, a quiet moan escaped my lips. My eyes went wide—and Dr. Campbell's hands hesitated for just a moment. *Shit!* He'd noticed it. And that meant that everyone around me had noticed, too.

Someone knock me out with a trowel so I can preserve at least a modicum of dignity, please!

"Owww!" I howled. Suddenly, his examination didn't feel as enjoyable. Sharp pain radiated above my foot where his finger touched.

He nodded to himself. "I think it might just be a sprain. Nothing seems to be broken."

Thank God for that, but the pain still wouldn't dissipate after he had pressed on the exact location of the injury.

I wiped away a trail of sweat from dripping down my forehead. Lying still in the hot sun somehow felt more intolerable than moving around. The rays scorched my skin, making me feel like I had a fever. Or maybe it was from all the unwanted attention I was receiving.

Dr. Campbell's deep blue eyes focused on my slick forehead. Without another word, he leaned in and with smooth force, he lifted me into his arms.

Oh, God. What was he doing?! *Please, no.*

The crowd parted for him.

"No, please. You don't have to carry me." I slipped my good foot to the floor and balanced on it, while attempting to rest the sprained one on the ground. I winced on contact and stumbled forward into him. The pain was excruciating, but there was no way in hell I was letting him carry me like a baby.

"Stubborn," was all he grunted out before sweeping me back up into his arms and stalking to the tent, not giving me much of a say in the matter. Out of the corner of my eye, I saw an amused Angela with brows nearly flying off her forehead. The bitch was loving my torment.

I tried hard to focus on anything but my mentor's hand just under my ass. His intention wasn't inappropriate, but since I was too well endowed with the gift of ass, his touch was dangerously close to being obscene.

My height was average, but Dr. Campbell carried me with ease, like I weighed as much as a feather. My body swayed rhythmically in his arms with every step he took.

He was silent as he walked with me, and I couldn't decide if this made the situation more or less awkward. So, I followed his lead and kept my mouth shut. *When in Rome...or in the arms of a man who looked like a Roman god . . .*

Gently, perhaps more so than I would have expected from a hard-ass like him, Dr. Campbell placed me onto the ground. I felt instant relief from the sun under the big white top.

I watched him pull out a red sack from the utility carrier. *A first-aid kit.* Using his free hand, he grabbed at a stainless steel water bottle and shoved it at me.

"Thanks." I drank from it greedily, liquid cooling my parched throat. The level of thirst one developed out here was unreal. It felt like no amount of water could ever fully hydrate you.

My love affair with the water bottle ended as soon as I felt warm hands take hold of my bare foot again. Startled, I jumped from the contact.

"Is the pain worsening?" he asked, propping the heel of my foot on his thigh as he sat cross-legged in front of me. His fingers moved to my arch to position it properly, resulting in an indescribable twist inside of my core.

I tried to play down my reaction. "No, no. Just on edge from the fall, I guess."

He nodded. "Must be the adrenaline from the injury."

Sure. The brooding professor touching my foot had nothing to do with it. I liked his explanation way better.

His hands unrolled the fat wad of nude elastic bandage as his eyes focused on mine. "You need better shoes."

I sighed. "I know, but the airline hasn't found my bag yet." I had been on the phone with them every free moment I had back at the hostel, but from the tone of the representative I had last spoken to, it seemed like I was chasing a lost cause.

"Then go buy new ones." His answer was blunt.

"You don't exactly leave us with much free time after work."

That caught his attention and he stared at me, perplexed. "What do you mean? We pack up and leave at sunset. You have the evening to do errands."

I choked on my laugh. He had to have been kidding. Not even he could be such a workaholic. The sun set at damn near 7 p.m., then it took almost an hour to drive back to the hostel. Whatever little time we got to ourselves, we used to eat and sleep.

"Why is that funny?" His expression remained flat as he rested his hands on my foot, which felt too intimate for our relationship as professor and student. Had I known someone would be up close and personal with my feet like this, I would have taken some time to get a pedicure before I'd flown here.

"It takes us nearly forty-five minutes to drive back to the hostel. And by the time we reach home, we barely have enough energy to eat and shower."

"It shouldn't be surprising that archaeology is hard work," he replied sternly. He began wrapping the bandage tightly around my ankle. Those damn cords in his tanned forearms flexed as he worked. "I outlined what this internship would involve."

It was obvious that he had forgotten what it was like being a student just starting out. I let out a sigh. "We're all certainly excited for this opportunity, but for most of us, this is the first time we've ever been on-site. This experience is new to us, and we're all trying our best."

His head reared up from my injury. Blue eyes blazed. "Are you telling me how to mentor my students?" His voice rumbled, like rage was just about to bubble over.

"What? No!" I tried desperately to smooth the situation over. "I just meant that we're all working really hard."

Dr. Campbell's hands jerked angrily as he quickly finished wrapping my ankle. He rose suddenly, and my foot dropped like an overripe coconut. He towered over me as I looked up at him from the ground. "If you want to get anywhere in life, you have to work. You might be used to a life of privilege where you come from, but look around you. This isn't sunny California where you can just clock in and out before lounging by the pool. This is the desert. There is no time to play out here, unless you're looking to join the dead bodies under the sand. I didn't get where I am today by being lazy and complaining about my schedule to my mentor. Handle your business on your own time like an adult without whining." He glared down his nose at me.

Heat pulsed through my cheeks and blood roared in my ears. I had never felt myself get this angry before. In fact, I'd always been known as the one who could remain calm under stress. But I was done—done with his judgment and condescension. I was done with being treated like his personal assistant.

My hands felt along the ground to find the balance to push myself up onto my good foot. He was still nearly a foot taller than me when I was standing, but I wasn't scared of him vand his tongue-lashing. "If you're going to make assumptions about me, then I get to make them about you, mentor or not."

My voice had come out louder than I'd expected; I might as well have been shouting in his face. I was certain the entire work crew was standing by, listening to every bit of our exchange. "You're an arrogant prick who gets off on making people feel lesser than you. You might be at the top of your field, but you're the bottom of the barrel when it comes to human beings. Maybe hanging out with dead people all day suits you, because you have no business spreading your toxicity to the living."

His face looked like I had just slapped him, nostrils flared and eyes wide in shock. Shock that someone had dared to speak to his majesty that way.

I could take a lot and smile through it. Dr. Campbell had been an asshole to me from the moment we'd met. But here he was calling me lazy and privileged, while the whole time I had been trying to tough out this internship with literally the clothes on my back. I didn't want a gold medal for enduring my shaky start, but I deserved some respect.

His throat worked as he swallowed, digesting my retort. Then he leaned in, his lips hovering inches from my own. "You want more free time?" His voice came out more like a hiss than a whisper. "Then consider yourself suspended."

He stomped away, clenched fists at his sides.

I stood there stunned, the ache in my foot nowhere near comparable to that in my chest. *What the fuck did I just do?*

Chapter 7

"I can't believe I was such an idiot!"

"I'm sure it's not as bad as you think, sweetheart." Mom was usually good at talking me off the ledge, but not this time. Instead, I felt myself getting more worked up as we spoke. It wasn't that she was irritating me; I was just too heated reliving the whole debacle.

"Mom, I called him a *prick*!"

"Correction: an *arrogant* prick," Angela quipped as she walked into our hostel room after serving her jail sentence under Warden Campbell's iron fist at the site. She loved recalling details from my humiliation any chance she had. *Friend vacancy still open. Only requirement is that you let me borrow your clothes.*

"Is that my Angela?" Mom's voice echoed through speakerphone. It was eight in the evening my time, which meant Mom was most likely on her lunch hour. The time difference was a bit frustrating when it came to staying in contact, but now that I was on suspension, I was free as a bird, though I hadn't had a chance to call her before now because I had been rushed off to the clinic to see a doctor about my ankle soon after my blowup with Dr. Campbell. And then I'd spent much of the next day sleeping off the pain medication.

"Hey, Ms. T! How's it going?" Angela shouted from her bed as she undid the laces of her boots.

"Not too bad. Missing you girls. The house is quiet without you around."

"Oh, please! You know you're throwing wild parties without us," Angela teased.

Mom chuckled. "You caught me. All male models, all day. With tiny banana hammocks."

"Mom!" I exclaimed.

"What?! Mothers need love, too!" Mom shot back.

We all broke out into laughter.

Angela called out, "Okay, Ms. T. I need to go shower. You wouldn't believe the crevices that sand can reach."

Mom had never changed her last name from Taha after Baba passed away. Her excuse was that it made the logistics of school pick-ups and healthcare visits easier if she shared the same last name as me. But I knew it was more than that, like she wasn't ready to let him go even though it had been decades.

"Okay, dear, you take care. Nice talking to you," Mom called out to Angela.

"You, too. Bye!" And with that, Angela left with her shower caddy and towel.

"So, what are you going to do about the 'arrogant prick'?" Mom asked, redirecting the conversation.

"Ugh, I don't know. It was so bad! He made me feel insignificant, and I just lost it."

I had checked my email on the hostel computer nearly every hour today, dreading that I'd receive a termination message from the internship coordinator. But nothing had ever shown up.

"First off, I'm proud of you for standing up for yourself, but I have to admit that this is very unlike you. You're usually so calm, and to a fault." Mom had always advocated for me to stand up for myself more, but I was typically too afraid to deal with confrontation.

My shoulders sagged with the weight of the reality that I had royally pissed off my mentor, likely to the point of no return. "I know. There's just something about Dr. Campbell that irks me."

"Is it because he's younger than you had probably imagined and in a position to boss you around?" she asked.

I shook my head. "I don't think so. He's still over ten years older than me." His age definitely wasn't the issue. And neither were his looks, not that I'd noticed them or anything. He was just an ass.

"From my perspective, he's a spring chicken," Mom replied.

"You're not old, Mom." She was only fifty-five but could pass for someone in her early forties. *Here's hoping those genes work in my favor, too!*

"I didn't say I was. But I have eyes, and your jerk of a professor is a *hottie.*"

"Please stop." Hearing my mom call my professor a "hottie" was too much to handle this late in the evening. Mom barely dated, so it always threw me off when she spoke about men. I wished she would find someone to settle down with.

"I just think that you don't like the unexpected as much as you think you do, and maybe seeing someone like Dr. Campbell in a position of power threw you off your game. But I still don't think you have anything to apologize for, no matter how caught off guard you were. Maybe you should talk to your professor and at least smooth things over. Hopefully, when he speaks to you, he'll realize how levelheaded you are and that he really was being an arrogant prick."

"I doubt that. He's so full of himself. Thinks he's God or something and that we're all his bitches."

"Most men in high positions are like that, regardless of their age. Imagine how many Dr. Campbells I've had to deal with during my career, especially when I first started. They expect women to be submissive and fall in line."

Even today, tech was a "bro industry" filled with men. Sure, companies were making more of an effort to include women at the table, but the field was still overwhelmingly male. I could only imagine how tough it must have been for Mom to have fought her way up the ladder so many years ago.

Archaeology was sadly the same. The field was full of men, and the few women who were permitted to work on-site bore the brunt of glares and sexist remarks. Even the bathroom provisions catered to men who could stand and piss anywhere they pleased. Some sites had porta potties, but they were too disgusting for females to use because no one cleaned them and they lacked toilet paper. At our site, we had to take a car to a nearby market and use the facilities there. It was a hassle to have someone drive you to use the restroom, and it was embarrassing to announce that you had to leave to pee to everyone on the site. Most women ended up holding their urine for far too long and would suffer chronic UTIs precipitated by dehydration, full bladders, and hot climates.

And God forbid you got your period on-site. There was nowhere to hide in the desert to change your tampon or even dispose of it. Most women, this one included, ended up going on the pill to control their cycles so that they wouldn't get their period while on excavation.

It was unfair, but I couldn't see this kind of thing changing anytime soon as long as men were in charge.

My voice prickled with irritation. "Are you saying you want me to go to him with my tail tucked between my legs?"

"No, not at all. You did the right thing by defending yourself. He was out of line, but at the same time, your career is a game. And you have to play it smartly. As far as I see it, you have two options: drop out of this internship and try for another one, or talk this out with Dr. Campbell to see if you can come to an understanding."

Dropping out wasn't a possibility. It was too late into the season to find another internship to meet my field requirement for the summer. I would have to spend an extra year in school just to make up for this internship. And if I left, it would stain my record for all future internships I applied to.

I huffed out an exhausted sigh. "I guess I need to talk to him."

"It's a good sign that he hasn't expelled you yet," Mom replied, her voice softening. "So maybe he's holding back on doing something extreme. Take advantage of that and go talk to him soon before he changes his mind."

Tomorrow was Friday and everyone had the day off, but Dr. Campbell would be on-site. Maybe I could catch him when he was alone and straighten this all out. We didn't need to get along, but maybe I could just tough it out for the next few weeks and then pack my shit up and go home.

My ego surrendered. "I'll talk to him."

"You got this, honey," Mom reassured me. "Don't let that asshole steal your shine."

I smiled. Mom was the toughest fighter I knew, and I was her daughter. That had to count for something. I wouldn't go down so easily. "I won't, Mom."

"That's my girl. How's your ankle feeling now?"

"The doctor said that it was just a mild sprain and to ice and rest it as much as I could." I was healing pretty quickly and could stand to put a little weight on it for small amounts of time without the use of the crutches the doctor had prescribed.

"Did you get new shoes?" Her tone held more warning than curiosity.

"Yeah, the owner of the hostel took pity on me and loaned me a pair of second-hand tennis shoes from his sister." They weren't in the best condition, but I was more than grateful to Asif for something that offered more support when I walked.

"Oh, that was nice of him," Mom chirped. "Listen, sweetheart. My lunch is about over, and I need to get back to work."

I hated having to hang up, but I couldn't keep her on the line forever. "Love you, Mom."

"Love you, too. Call me tomorrow?"

"It's a date."

"I miss you," she said, sadness coating her voice.

I blinked back my homesick tears. "Miss you, too." More than she could imagine. Now was the time I wished I had my mommy here to hold my hand—I needed all the support before facing the big bad wolf tomorrow.

Chapter 8

On a regular work day, the site was teeming with activity: workers hollering and laughing loudly, baskets being thrown about, metal clanking against rock.

But not today. Friday was the holy day of the week on which Muslims congregated at their local mosques and prayed together late in the afternoon. As a courtesy, the Ministry of Antiquities recommended that workers be given the option to have the day off. The discretion was left up to the director of each excavation, and it seemed that Dr. Campbell had been generous enough to offer the option to his team. *Shocking.*

I wished I could have said that Dr. Campbell's unbelievable generosity was responsible for the internship team having Saturdays off, too, but it was due to policy set by the program.

The site was eerily quiet. I took in the white tent still standing with all of the tools and cheaper equipment inside, and the small craters in the sand left by the caravan of bodies that had traversed the lot. It was like witnessing a ghost town that had once boasted life in its past...twice, actually. Ancient ghosts mixed with recent ghosts.

If I hadn't noticed the Jeep parked out front where the shuttle had dropped me, I would have assumed Dr. Campbell was just a ghost of the past too. At least, I wished he was.

I couldn't see him anywhere in the distance, so he was most likely inside of the temple. Or maybe the ancient Egyptian gods had taken mercy on my plight and decided to do me a solid by burying him in quicksand...I sighed. The prospect was highly unlikely. A girl could dream, though.

The shuttle engine roared to life behind me before zooming away in the sweltering sun.

Deserted in the desert. I wasn't really alone, but that would have been more preferable than being in the company of Dr. Grump. *Too bad.* If I wanted to protect everything I had worked so hard for, I didn't have a choice in the matter.

Steeling my spine, I moved forward through the sand. My ankle still ached a little, but I had wrapped it securely earlier to give it some extra support. The used tennis shoes allowed me to move comfortably with a slight limp, but I had still brought along my crutches for added assistance. I didn't plan to stay for long; the shuttle would be back in an hour to pick me up. I just needed some time to say my piece.

My heart was racing as my feet trudged forward atop grit and gravel, with my Waterstones canvas bag over my shoulder. Every step slower than the last, I was dreading the moment I'd face the *arrogant prick*. My blood heated all over again thinking of how he'd berated me. This morning, I had resolved to retain my composure and essentially plaster on my best imitation of a pageant smile as I begged for my internship spot back. I hadn't been expelled from the program yet, but having no return date from suspension was as good as expulsion.

The thought of groveling in front of this insufferable man made bile rise up my throat. I'd rather undergo an ancient Egyptian root canal sans sedative. But my career depended on having this internship. I didn't want to be held back another year for not fulfilling my requirements, nor did I want to have to explain why I didn't complete a once-in-a-lifetime opportunity under the king of Egyptology.

The entrance of the temple was free of the plywood that was used to keep it shut, and the faint glow of light shone through the entryway, indicating that someone was inside. *The Blond-Haired Ogre.*

Rolling my shoulders back and tipping my chin high, I focused my anger, turning it into determination. Determination to get what I wanted out of this. An apology was too far-fetched to expect, but I wanted my intern spot. He owed me that much for speaking to me the way that he had.

I parked my crutches outside on the ground and hobbled inside.

My eyes took a moment to adjust to the dimness.

There he was, crouching on the ground over shards of rock and broken pottery. Instead of launching straight into my rehearsed attempt for a second chance, I stood there observing him. I could only see his profile from where I stood. His hands clutched at his overgrown locks. I'd bet that when he wasn't on a dig, he kept his hair groomed and trimmed short, but this unkempt style was more intriguing to look at.

A flashlight was propped on a plastic fold-out table beside him to serve as overhead lighting while he worked. His eyes bounced from the artifacts in front of him to his opened notebook littered with scrawled handwriting.

Suddenly, he grabbed the notebook and hurled it about four feet ahead of him. Even in anger, he was careful not to harm the historic walls that encased him.

Large hands rubbed at his face, a cloud of frustration surrounding him. He no longer looked like the pain-in-the-ass professor that I loathed; instead,

I saw a like a tormented man. Like his insecurities were demons that haunted him.

I held my breath as I stood frozen, unsure of what to do. My brain warned me that I should turn around and skip the talk altogether to avoid having something chucked at my head.

But a feeling in my core urged me to stay, to comfort him. To tell him that everything would be alright, even though I hated him.

My feet felt leaden as I struggled to decide whether I wanted to go to him or retreat, causing me to stumble when I finally took a step forward. Rocks rolled from my tumble, capturing Dr. Campbell's attention.

He stood up hastily, startled that the safety of his loneliness had been breached. He squinted in my direction, the natural sunlight through the entrance marring his vision. "Sanura?"

My hand flashed a wave as casually as I could muster, but I probably just looked like I was shooing away a fly. "Hey, Dr. Campbell. How's it going?" My voice was even more awkward than my wave.

"What are you doing here?" he asked, bewildered.

I limped fully into the temple. I had been inside briefly during my day-and-a-half stint as an archaeology intern, but never really had a chance to explore. The interior was small, looking more like a utility closet than an ancient place of worship. One would only be able to tell it was a shrine from the hieroglyphs and carved statues of Tutankhamun set along the wall.

"I was wondering if we could maybe talk. About the other day." My fingers fiddled in front of my waist.

"I see." His eyes pierced mine with intensity.

"I haven't heard anything about an end date for my suspension, and I hoped that—"

He raised his hand to stop me—a condescending move, but I let him have it.

"You can come back."

My mouth gaped open. I'd been expecting to fight for my position or at the very least offer a fake apology. Never had I thought that I would merely have to utter a few sentences and get to return without discussing what was said.

His analytical stare fell to my ankle, scanning it over. "What's the matter? You're staring at me like that wasn't what you wanted."

"I mean...it is. No, it's what I want," I stammered. "I just thought you'd need an apology or something."

His focus flashed to my face, making my breath hitch. "Apologies are bullshit. People tell them all the time without ever meaning them. They're like magic empty words people use when they selfishly want to move on. It bears no consequence for the person receiving the apology."

"I guess that's one way to put it." He kind of had a point. Apologies were often just a formality and didn't hold much meaning. Mine certainly wouldn't have.

"Did you come all the way here to offer me an empty apology?" One of his thick eyebrows hiked expectantly at me.

I tested his patience. "Would you rescind your decision for me to return if I said yes?"

He chuckled, catching me by surprise again. "I wouldn't. Were you expecting me to apologize to you for the things I said?"

Honestly, I was. He was out of line, and I was hoping that he regretted his premature judgment of me. "Your assessment of me was wrong. I don't think it was fair for you to say those things, not just about me but the other interns."

His jaw worked as he considered my words. Dr. Campbell listened without interrupting me, though I couldn't tell what he was thinking from his poker face. I moved closer to him, catching an aroma of something aged, like a mix of leather-bound books and whiskey.

"This excavation is probably just one of many for you," I continued, "but it's my first taste of being in the field, doing what I plan to devote my entire career to."

"You're wrong," he replied bluntly.

"What?"

So low that I could barely catch what he said, almost like he was regretting his admission as he was saying it, he muttered, "This isn't just another excavation for me. This one matters to me more than you know."

My eyes traveled to the splayed-out notebook on the ground, searching for a more substantial explanation. "Care to share?"

He turned away from me and carefully collected his notes, straightening the pages out, before bending over the samples he had been studying on the ground. "That's for me to worry about."

There was something big troubling him, but I doubted I would ever figure it out, nor would I ever get that apology I sought from him. He was a man of walls stronger than the ones that had housed this temple for thousands of years.

It was near time for me to head back to wait for the shuttle, but instead, I slipped my backpack off my shoulders and fished out my notebook and pen. I had brought them in case my confrontation went south and I needed to document it. Taking a seat on the ground, I faced the hieroglyphs on the wall and set to work on deciphering them. It was one thing to read them out of books or photos, but to see them in real life was astounding. The images in our textbooks benefited from camera features like zoom and focus. Seeing the images in real life, clustered together like an elaborate mosaic of history, was something completely different. It was harder to decipher them on aged stone where the figures were faint as a result of weathering.

"What are you doing?" Dr. Campbell was studying me quizzically from his stooped position.

"Curing the common cold. What does it look like?" I flashed a cheesy smile.

He stared at me incredulously. "You want to stay here on your day off?"

I couldn't help but nod eagerly. I had missed being on-site and now that I was back, there was no way I was being pushed away again.

All Dr. Campbell could offer in response was a shake of the head and a disbelieving grin.

"Any headway on figuring out who built this thing since I've been gone?" I asked, waving my hands in the air at the stone around us.

"None."

I grinned. "Maybe that's because I wasn't here to figure it out."

He smirked at my remark. He wasn't the only one who had an ego. I was tied with Angela for the top of our class and absorbed everything I learned like a sponge.

I turned my attention back to the wall of hieroglyphs before me. My pen found paper, sketching figures that I saw to create a clearer image so I could puzzle the bits of information together for easier reading. I was still new to this, so I couldn't read columns and columns of symbols like a seasoned expert could.

"Need any help making them out?" Dr. Campbell had taken a seat just behind me, his presence warming my back.

I looked over my shoulder, catching his interested expression. He was a handsome man by nature, but when he wasn't scowling, he looked downright dreamy. The kind of *dreamy* that had a girl seeing stars. Kind of like the ones I was seeing right now.

I blinked furiously to get them to stop rotating and flashing like in those old *Looney Tunes* cartoons where Pepé Le Pew kept ogling that poor black cat. "Um, sure."

"You probably already learned this, but hieroglyphs are meant to be read from right to left in the columns that they're inscribed in."

"I remember that from class."

He nodded. "We'd usually start reading this from the right-most part of the wall and complete each column as we moved right. But sometimes hieroglyphs can be written left to right, making it more confusing to decipher. One of the easiest ways to figure out the direction is to locate an animal symbol and read into its face." He leaned in close to me and pointed over my shoulder. "Do you recognize that symbol?"

It was a series of hieroglyphs inside of a rope. "It's a cartouche."

"That's right. Do you know what the rope represents?"

"It's used as protection for the name enclosed inside." Usually, it was used for the names of people deserving great respect, like pharaohs and queens.

"Smart girl."

His voice had dipped lower, and the compliment sent an unexplained shiver down my spine.

"Do you recognize the name inside?"

I did. It was arguably one of the most well-known names of all of ancient Egypt. "Tutankhamun." It wasn't written out phonetically in hieroglyphs, but if you pieced together the syllables, you could deduce his name.

"Beautiful." His warm breath tickled the back of my neck. Involuntarily, my body leaned ever so slightly closer.

I continued reading. "The first three symbols resembling a reed, a small checkerboard, and a zig-zagged line represent the god of creation."

"*Amun,*" he clarified while nodding.

It was exciting to see this side of him, encouraging me and not ready to rip anything I said to shreds. I almost felt like I was on one of those highs you get when you hit a breakthrough while writing an essay or taking an exam.

My eyes jumped to the next line. "The bird with the two loaves of bread means '*Tut*.'"

"Keep going," he urged, his voice even quieter than before and tickling the nerve endings in my earlobe.

I moved onto the cross with a loop on top. "That's the *ankh*. It represents life."

"Good girl," he hummed.

My breath hitched at his praise. I wanted whatever this was to keep going, to keep earning his approval.

"And what about the last line?"

I examined the crook at the bottom right, which I knew to signify a ruler since every pharaoh was pictured with it. The next two symbols looked too faint for me to identify. They were long and the last I recognized as a plant, or a flower. I was too distracted to remember, but I wracked my brain anyway, trying to place it. Then it came to me, and I spun to face him. "King of Wisdom!"

"Well done." The look of satisfaction on Dr. Campbell's face seared my cheeks with heat.

Diverting my gaze, I twirled the pen in my hand. "Thanks."

"Care to show me what else you know?" he asked expectantly.

My eyes darted back to his. My throat felt thick, yet I couldn't read anything lewd in his expression. *Get a grip, Kitty! He meant your stellar hieroglyph-reading skills!*

For some odd reason, disappointment slumped through me, and my core, which had been clenched tightly with anticipation, released in defeat.

Still, I forced the corners of my lips to tip upward as I turned back toward the wall of symbols. "Sure."

Chapter 9

The second week of the internship flew by smoother. And the best part was that I was in attendance every day. *Glory to God and all of his anointed pharaohs*, or whatever prayer was fitting for digging up mummies.

My ankle felt even better, and I could put weight onto it for longer periods of time, though the group wouldn't let me carry anything heavier than a hand shovel. One time, Dr. Campbell caught me carrying a basket of debris to toss into the waste pile and promptly ripped it out of my hands and admonished me for doing too much. In fact, the dynamics between us had completely shifted ever since we'd spent that day alone together in the temple. He had eased up on me considerably—I'd even gotten a "Good morning" yesterday. However, though I felt more comfortable with my mentor, I was still careful around him because something told me he was as mercurial as the summer days were long.

Sitting cross-legged about five yards from the temple with my ass planted on the ground, I was busy combing through the sand with a brush. I had cleared away some of the surface sand and rock using a hand trowel first, discarding nearly two feet of debris.

I had a sneaking suspicion that this temple had been built by a woman. Most temples built by pharaohs boasted monuments and hieroglyphs that painted the royal in a strong and very masculine light. This was because the pharaohs had commissioned the priests and builders to do so. They would basically spoon-feed the self-serving compliments that ended up on the walls. Even the statues could be intimidating in size—they were possibly the biggest show of small-dick syndrome one could ever witness.

However, while reviewing the hieroglyphs with Dr. Campbell, I'd noticed the description of Tutankhamun was softer and more nurturing than usually used to depict a pharaoh. For example, scenes from Tutankhamun's burial chamber discovered by Howard Carter in 1922 painted him as a seasoned combatant riding his chariot, even though we now know that he was merely a teenager for most of his rule. He'd even been buried with a dagger made of meteorite material as a show of his power. Like he was a warrior god.

But on the walls of this temple, scenes of the young king were painted in a much different light than I had seen in textbooks. *More human.* His childhood was etched out in detail: A young boy playing in a garden with his sisters. A child seated at his father's feet during Akhenaten's reign. Another image of Tutankhamun alongside his wife, Ankhesenamun. There was only one scene where he was seated on a throne, holding the crook and flail as a woman was pictured kneeling at his feet, presumably his wife again.

There were a handful of notable women who had been close to Tutankhamun in his life. His biological mother, who some researchers believed to have been a woman named Kiya, was one of Akhenaten's many wives and also his full sister. It would have made for a touching hypothesis that his biological mother was the creator of this temple, but according to historical records, there was very little known about the woman. Could she have secretly commissioned a team to build this temple for her son?

Another more prominent woman of the king's past was his stepmother and Akhenaten's primary wife, Nefertiti. Most people would instantly recognize the famous queen whose bust had become a symbol of ancient Egyptian femininity and power. Could she have been the one to construct this temple for her stepson? It was definitely a possibility. She had the means and power to do so, more so than Tutankhamun's birth mother.

An interesting bit of information about Nefertiti was that she was believed to have been the daughter of Ay, one of Tutankhamun's advisers after he ascended to the throne as a young boy. However, after the death of Tutankhamun, Ay had fought for power and had become pharaoh himself. It seemed that he always had one eye on the throne, even while it was occupied. It was even believed that Ay had decided to bury Tutankhamun in a makeshift tomb while Ay reserved Tutankhamun's intended tomb for his own death. Ay's thirst for power had run deep, even into the afterlife. Where had Nefertiti stood in all of this? Had her allegiance belonged to her father or her stepson?

Tutankhamun was believed to have had six sisters, all of them the daughters of Nefertiti and Akhenaten, making them his half-sisters since they only shared the same father. Of all the sisters, only one was mentioned multiple times in historical records. *Ankhesenamun.* Tutankhamun's wife. The pair had been wed when they were only children. Ankhesenamun had become a widow after her husband passed away when he was only nineteen years old. Her story is a common one of most queens who find themselves without a husband.

It was said that when Ay secured the throne, he forced Ankhesenamun, his alleged own granddaughter, to marry him. There was evidence that Ankhesenamun tried to prevent the marriage from happening based on a letter she sent to a neighboring ruler, begging to marry one of his sons for protection. It would have been strange for an Egyptian queen to consider a foreign marriage in those times, which was why it was believed that she had been fearful of the marriage to Ay. But following Ay's ascension to the throne, very little of the possibly two-time queen was known.

Tutankhamun didn't have any surviving children, so the hypothesis that it was one of them who'd built the temple in his honor was false.

I hadn't brought up my theory about the patron yet to Dr. Campbell, mostly because my brain seemed to be malfunctioning anytime he was nearby. I chalked it up to his superficial good looks and nothing more. The man could catch the eye of a blind chimpanzee, with his perfectly symmetrical face.

I refused to be the poor school girl crushing on her professor like another romance novel cliché.

My eyes still couldn't help but roam to him standing in front of the tent, though. He seemed to be deep in discussion with Isabella. One week, and she had already secured her spot as my least favorite person on the team. Whenever any one of us would answer one of Dr. Campbell's pop quiz questions, she'd rip apart our responses and supply her own dissertation for a question that had originally warranted a one-word answer. The girl was the first to climb over us to get to Dr. Campbell the second he was alone. And the most irritating part of it was that she assumed she was always right.

The demographics of our internship weren't normal. Three females and only two males had been selected to participate in a dig. An *all-male* dig. There were no females on Dr. Campbell's team, so I supposed in the grand scheme of things, Isabella was just commanding respect in an already biased field. I just wished she wasn't so annoying in the way she went about it. Shit, at least be a little nicer to the other two girls on the team instead of treating us like competition!

I watched their exchange. Isabella's mouth moved a mile a minute, while Dr. Campbell stood in front of her, patiently waiting for her to stop for air. His facial features remained relaxed as if unaffected by her, but I knew otherwise: the way he slowly balled his hands at his side and then extended his fingers. The way his back arched slightly like a lion provoked one too many times. I knew he was just itching to get away from her.

He wasn't a man of many words, nor did he like to listen to them. I was still surprised at how many he had shared with me inside of the temple. The moment should have felt awkward, yet it hadn't. In fact, my body had filled with warmth whenever he'd urged me to continue. He was obviously passionate about his work since he was a prominent figure in the field, but to see him light up as he helped me read basic hieroglyphs had been completely unexpected. The feeling was like a drug, and I wanted more of it.

"You guys seem like you're getting along now." Felipe's cheerful voice ripped my focus from Dr. Campbell. His smile was gentle as he crouched down onto the ground next to me.

"Yeah, I guess I magically got less annoying to him since last week." I smirked as I continued brushing away the sand to expose more rock underneath.

Felipe took hold of one of the available brushes on the ground next to me and mimicked my motions. "You're not annoying. He's just a penis," he said flatly in his thick Spanish accent.

My brush ceased its job and I stared back at him wide-eyed. "You mean *a dick*?"

"Yes, a dick," he confirmed.

My belly rumbled with laughter, and the sound that came out of my mouth bellowed around me.

Felipe joined me, chuckling. "You had better quiet down. The *dick* is looking at us."

My eyes caught Dr. Campbell's intense glare, which strangled my laughter.

"I take it that your conversation went well with him, since your suspension seems to be old news?" Felipe asked as we continued brushing.

I kept my answer short. "Words were exchanged, but I'm not sure how much of an effect they had."

"They must have worked. He seems to be more tolerant of the rest of us, too."

"Well, at least some good came from my outburst," I teased.

"You were right for putting him in his place. The things he said to you were out of line."

I didn't like that news of our heated exchange had spread through the site like wildfire, but I was glad I wasn't the only one who thought my feelings were valid. "I just didn't like being called lazy."

"You're anything but lazy." He brushed my cheek with his fingers.

My hand flew to the spot he had touched as I gaped back at him. His touch had been soft...gentle...but had felt foreign to me.

"Sand," he answered bluntly.

"Oh." I brushed the spot off some more.

Felipe stared at me like he wanted to say something, but I diverted my gaze before he could continue. Whatever it was, I felt like I wasn't ready to hear it.

My brush worked furiously at the earth in front of me. Something hard prevented me from digging deeper.

I dipped my head closer to inspect the area. *Blue.* A small speck of vibrant blue below the khaki-colored sand.

"What? What's wrong?" Felipe asked.

"There's something here," I gritted out as I moved away the sand that concealed it with my trowel instead.

"Here, let me help." Felipe began working alongside me to brush the debris away.

More blue stone was revealed with our efforts. Small box-shaped gems glistened under the sunlight. I reached for the trowel and pushed it under the sand holding the item and gently lifted. The object finally dislodged from the earth and sat atop the trowel.

"Holy shit," Felipe gasped in amazement. "What is it?" He leaned in so close our foreheads nearly touched.

Tiny slabs of deep blue shined back at me from my tool. Thin brown strings ran through holes in the tops and bottoms of each slab, stringing the slabs together. The strings appeared to be made of leather, and one of the tails had a knot tied into it, like it was used as a closure. At the end of another of the tails was a silver medallion, murky from natural deterioration over time. I examined the face of the medallion. The etched design was difficult to see, and I squinted to make out the insignia. *A wreath of flowers.*

"I think it's a bracelet," I breathed out. It was beautiful but unlike anything I had seen before.

Felipe jumped up suddenly and waved his hands. "Dr. Campbell, come quick!" he shouted.

Our mentor jogged over with an entourage in tow.

"Have you found something?" Mo barreled his way through the team, who all stood around in a huddle waiting expectantly. "Show me."

Dr. Campbell stooped beside me, his expression bland as if he weren't willing to get his hopes up just yet, unlike the others who crowded around us. Without a word, his eyes flashed to mine.

I gingerly lifted the delicate object with the end of my brush and placed it in my palm. His fingers shocked my sensitive skin to life as he lifted the item, the grains of sand tickling my flesh from his contact. His eyebrows narrowed. I could see the wheels in his head turning as he examined the button clasp.

"James?" Mo prodded impatiently.

I held my breath, waiting for his assessment. My heart thumped loudly against my ribcage.

Dr. Campbell rolled stones between his fingers. "The gems seem to be authentic lapis lazuli. But I can't quite place what this metal is." His thumb stroked the smooth metal of the flower button.

"What time period?" Mo asked, swiping at the sweat on his bald head with a washcloth before replacing his straw hat on top.

Dr. Campbell lifted the bracelet to examine it in the sunlight. "Seems to be New Kingdom. Most likely eighteenth dynasty."

That would have placed it in the time of the temple's construction.

"Where do you think it came from?" Felipe asked.

"I'm not certain, but could be from someone with stature based on the excellent quality of the stones."

"Like the patron of this temple?" I asked.

Dr. Campbell's gaze deepened into mine for the briefest of seconds. So brief that the onlookers wouldn't have noticed. "Perhaps. Or maybe even the priest of this temple."

It had been common for both men and women in ancient Egypt to wear jewelry. But judging from the circumference of the bracelet, I guessed it had belonged to a woman. *My theory still held strong—for now!*

"Mo, let's get this to the lab to identify the metal," he said.

Mo nodded eagerly. "I will have one of the men drive it over immediately."

"And, Sanura?"

My chest tightened at my name on his lips. "Yes, Dr. Campbell?"

"Great job." One corner of his mouth lifted into the faintest semblance of a smile. It might not have been a full, gleaming one of appreciation, but it was just as comparable for me. Air filled my diaphragm as I beamed with pride.

Outwardly, I offered him a smile, as professional as I could muster, in return. "Thank you, Dr. Campbell."

Before I could register what was happening, I was pulled to my feet and enveloped in thick arms. Felipe's squeeze was tight around my torso. "Congratulations! The first find of the internship!"

I pulled away from him shyly, and tucked stray hair behind my ears to distract from my heated cheeks. "Thanks."

The entire crew seemed to be surprised by Felipe's display of affection, especially one member in particular.

Dr. Campbell's glare blazed against my skin hotter than the desert sun. The cord in the side of his neck twitched as his eyes remained trained on Felipe and me. My recently found excitement instantly vanished and unease rattled my core.

Chapter 10

The clouds parted and the heavens shined forth for all to rejoice. You heard right! *My luggage was found!*

I had lost all hope of ever recovering my belongings before God, the devil, or magic (pick your favorite poison) had done me a solid and prompted Sara from Baggage Support to call me last night. They'd arranged for a courier to deliver my bag this morning, and I swear on all things pumpkin spice, I victory-danced around the hostel lobby for two minutes straight when it arrived. Asif, the hostel manager, was highly amused by my lack of rhythm.

All my things were back in my possession: my clothes that weren't two sizes too small, my shoes that fit without slipping off my feet, my archaeology notes, my scant supply of toiletries and makeup, and most importantly, my laptop.

I had put off one of my main reasons for accepting the internship for too long: finding my uncle. Sure, I could have used my phone to start the search, but I hated working on such a small screen.

Luckily, it was our day off and I could spare as much time as I needed to search for my uncle today. I found a café within walking distance and headed out with my laptop.

The reviews didn't disappoint. The café was adorable. Colorful mosaics made of tile adorned the walls and beautiful terracotta pots decorated the interior. It was one of those places that seemed to have been established just for the hordes of visitors who journeyed to Luxor hoping to catch a glimpse of a cursed mummy.

The café was quiet, with only a few customers scattered around the seating area. Some had their laptops with them like me and were busy typing away—perhaps students from the nearby university.

I sipped my cardamom-flavored coffee and began scouring the Internet. A basic Google search on "How to find people living in Egypt?" brought up sites on which others had already posed the same question. I wasn't alone shooting in the dark and trying to come up with gold.

The most popular response seemed to suggest the best way was to post on various social forums, so I set to work hitting as many of the recommended platforms as I could. Wouldn't it be awesome if someone replied to my thread and I ended up finding my uncle?!

I wondered what he would look like. Most of my appearance came from Baba, except for my freckles, which came from Mom. Maybe I would resemble my uncle, too; they were brothers, after all.

The thought that excited me the most was the hope that my uncle had children of his own. I might finally have cousins to bond with. I was an only child, and my mom only had one sister who had never had children of her own, leaving me pretty lonely for my entire upbringing. No family slumber parties, no kids' table at Thanksgiving, no one to sneak out of the house with when I got my driver's license. Don't get me wrong, it wasn't a bad childhood, just very different from the ones my friends had experienced.

But the thought that I might have other living and breathing family members who were around my age made my stomach flutter with excitement. And maybe they even had kids of their own. I could be an aunty and not even know it!

I clicked furiously, finding every site that I could. I even posted onto Reddit in hopes that something would turn up.

I was so focused that I barely registered the group of guys pulling up chairs to my table until they were all seated.

I looked up nervously, brushing away a loose curl that had fallen into my face. "Ummm...hi."

"Ah, she finally noticed us," said the bleach-blond guy in a soccer jersey to his cronies. His skin was fair, with evidence of a sunburn on the tip of his pointy nose. Judging from his accent, he seemed to be European.

"I'm sorry, but can I help you?" I asked, my gut telling me that I didn't want to know his answer.

"An American, too," Peroxide Hair snickered.

What did that have to do with anything?

The grin on the guy to his left, a man with jet-black hair and a goatee, made my scalp prickle in response. "No, but maybe we can help you? A pretty girl like you shouldn't be alone."

"I'm not sure what you need, but I should be going," I answered hastily. I shut my laptop and stood, ready to toss it into my bag, when Black Hair's hand pressed it back down onto the table.

"Where are you rushing off to? Stay and let's get to know each other." The veins in his forearms bulged from how firmly he was pressing my computer into the table.

The third guy sat back and cackled at his friend's move.

Panic pulsed through me. There were three guys and only one of me. They were much larger than me and would probably catch me if I bolted right now.

My eyes flashed just to my left, hoping to catch someone's eye for help, but all I saw was an older man who was engrossed in a book, paying us no attention.

Instead of showing fear, I plastered on a fake smile and somehow steadied my voice. "I really need to get going. I'm supposed to be meeting someone soon."

"I said, sit *down*." Black Hair grabbed my arm and forced me into the chair.

Oh, no. No, no, no. Fear gripped my throat like a fist as I yanked against his hold and shouted, "Let me go!"

"Why are you in such a hurry to get away? We're nice guys just looking to make new friends. Don't you want to be friends with us?" Peroxide Hair ground out.

My chest heaved trying to take in air, but it felt more like I was suffocating. Black Hair's grip on my arm wouldn't let up, his fingers squeezing into my flesh.

"Let her go," a thick voice rumbled behind me.

Black Hair released me, and I turned to find a fuming Dr. Campbell behind me.

My eyes went wide with surprise, but my mouth stayed mute. I had seen him angry before, but this was ten times worse than during our argument at the site.

"Relax, man." Peroxide Hair lifted his palms in the air. "We were just trying to get to know each other. We're all buddies here." His voice was disgustingly sardonic.

"I believe the lady told you she wasn't interested." Dr. Campbell's voice matched the strength of his stature. The cords in his arms were visible in the tightly stretched black T-shirt he wore, even though his hands were tucked into the pockets of his dark jeans. His hands must have been clenched to show that kind of definition. His broad shoulders towered over the rest of us at the table. But his eyes were the scariest part of him. Those deep blues raged with a fire that could burn down the entire building.

"Why don't you save yourself some trouble, old man." Peroxide Hair threw a wad of cash at Dr. Campbell's chest. "Go buy yourself a coffee and get lost." The three goons burst into cackles.

Faster than lightning, Dr. Campbell reached over the table and grabbed the ringleader's neck with his hands. I jumped back, my chair falling with a clatter behind me.

The other two guys backed away hastily.

His hands must have been squeezing tightly against Peroxide Hair's airway because all that came out of the asshole was a squeaking wheeze.

I held my breath as Dr. Campbell leaned in, his long torso stretching over the table. "Get. The. Fuck. Out. She's mine," he hissed into his victim's face.

With that, he tossed the asshole to the floor like he was a ball of paper—light and unimportant.

The other two helped their friend to his feet, and they ran out of the shop like a trio of hyenas being chased away by a lion.

They were gone. My whole body relaxed as I breathed out a sigh of relief. So grateful to Dr. Campbell, I approached him. "Thank you so much—"

"Pack your shit up and let's go," he growled.

I flinched at his unexpected anger. I had never really heard him swear before, even when he'd berated me at the site. Why was he still angry? The guys were gone, and he'd won!

Before I could ask him what was the matter, he barked at me again. "Now!"

With clumsy hands, I tucked my laptop into my bag. He grabbed my elbow and guided me to the front door, but not before I stuck my tongue out at the old man still absorbed in his book and the shop owner who had just stood behind the counter the whole time. *Waste-of-space men!*

When we reached outside, Dr. Campbell's hand was still on me, and his pace was too fast for me to keep up. "You can let go of me now. I'm totally fine."

"Keep walking," he ordered.

My feet stumbled as I tried to stop moving. "I can walk myself home." I pulled away from his grasp.

He turned to look at me, those deep blues still burning bright. "They could still be lurking around here. It's not safe for you to walk home alone."

I hadn't thought about that. I'd just assumed that the goons would have run away by now, since Dr. Campbell had served their asses to them. If I ran into them alone, there would be no hope of me escaping with how pissed they'd be.

So, I obeyed and followed him.

After about two minutes of hardcore power walking, I broke the silence. "Where are we going?"

"My place," he answered curtly while focusing on the street ahead.

"But why?" I protested. "My hostel is only five minutes away from here." He could just walk me home if he was that concerned about those guys following me.

But he didn't relent. "As is my home."

This was highly inappropriate and a little dramatic, if you asked me, but with the mood he was in, I wasn't willing to press my luck. Next thing you know, he'd go all *Mucha Lucha* on me like he had with Peroxide Hair, and I quite liked my neck.

So, I followed in his shadow, which was just as dark as his mood.

Chapter 11

The hostel stay was free during the course of the internship, but the average traveler would expect to pay around fifteen American dollars per night. According to some fast math in my head and what limited knowledge I had about Egyptian real estate, I'd have said that Dr. Campbell's hotel suite (nay, "penthouse") must have cost in the neighborhood of fifty thousand dollars per month to rent. (I could have been off, so feel free to add another ten thousand to that figure for good measure.)

Yes. It was that ~~grand~~. . . ~~lavish~~. . . opulent. Finding the right word to describe the museum-sized living space I stood in the center of at that very moment wasn't easy.

Black and gray furniture. Hanging glass orbs. Dark stone flooring. Modern staircase with gunmetal railings. Panoramic windows with the most breathtaking view of the Nile. This place was no ordinary penthouse, this was the ultimate man-palace.

I stood gaping at my surroundings, feeling severely underdressed in my T-shirt and jeans as Dr. Campbell was busy in the kitchen grabbing me the glass of water I had requested. The man had all but made me jog in the blazing heat to keep up with him, so the least he could do was get me a cold glass of water as compensation if he wasn't going to give me a good explanation as to why I had to hide out at his place instead of my own.

He returned with a sleekly designed glass that was definitely not the kind you could chug from, especially with a slice of lemon floating at the top of the water.

"Thanks," I said as I lifted the glass in the air as if to cheers him, even though he didn't have a drink for himself. All that earned me was a nod.

The awkwardness took hold again like it did whenever I was alone with Dr. Campbell. It was his gaze—always scrutinizing the person in front of him. Picking them apart and evaluating their flaws.

"Nice place you got here," I said, hoping small talk would ease the tension. "That's awesome that the grant committee put you up in a fancy suite like this."

"It's not a rental," he answered gruffly. "I own it."

My jaw nearly dropped to the floor. "Own?! Since when do archaeologists make bank?" The words fell out of my mouth before I could filter them, and I felt my eyes go wide. "Oh, jeez, I'm so sorry. I didn't mean it that way." He was a prodigy in the field, but even so, that wouldn't have warranted this kind of wealth.

"No offense taken," he replied blandly.

"I just meant that this place is so gorgeous, I'm shocked it would be available to buy since it's in a luxury hotel."

"True, but it was purchased during development, long before the hotel ever opened to residents in 1932."

The trendy penthouse certainly didn't scream 1930s style, so I assumed it had undergone a face lift or two over the ages to make it as contemporary as it was.

"Wow! Did you buy it off the previous owners?" I took a sip of the icy water in my hand.

"No, I inherited it." I could hear that near-constant edge of irritation in his voice growing thicker.

I wiggled my brows at him. "Ah, a rich boy." Only old money used words like "inherited."

He twisted his lips as if I had just told him his dog was ugly, if he were the type who was caring enough to own a pet. "By birth. And not by choice," he said, disgust rolling off him.

I lifted my free hand in surrender. "No judgment here. Just surprised, is all." With no intention of pressing the topic further, I put my glass down and picked up my bag. I had clearly overstayed my welcome, and I found my way to the door with every intention to leave.

But his voice stopped me in my tracks. "My grandfather was a fairly successful businessman." He strolled over to the windows, his back to me, as he spoke. "When he passed away, he left much of his estate to me, including this apartment."

Surprised by his openness, I dropped my bag and drifted toward his turned back. Dr. Campbell wasn't one to share personal information like this, and I was compelled by his honesty. "How did he pass away?"

His voice was quiet. "A heart attack right before I was accepted to university."

I could relate to losing a loved one to health reasons. "I'm sorry. Were you close?"

"We were. Much to my family's dismay. My parents were upset that he left me the bulk of his wealth and not them or my younger brother. But they never had really given a damn about my grandfather unless it came to his money."

That sounded awful, witnessing your own family being fake just to get money. "Do you talk to your family often?"

"No. Not since my grandfather died nearly twenty years ago."

"Shit," I whispered. Dr. Campbell looked over his shoulder at my expletive. I offered an apologetic smile. "Sorry. Mouth of a sailor." His eyes darted to my mouth, then he quickly turned to gaze back out the window.

I moved to his side to peer at the view of the rippling dark water.

"That's a long time not to speak to family," I continued.

Dr. Campbell remained silent.

"I wish I had a lot more family alive." It was a private confession that should never have escaped my lips, but for some reason, it had, and I couldn't take it back.

"No siblings?" His interest seemed genuine.

"None. Just my mother back at home. She has a sister, but my aunt never had children."

"What about your father?"

"I don't remember much of him, because he passed away from cancer when I was little."

"What type of cancer?"

"A brain tumor."

His lips tightened, my story clearly affecting him. "Any relatives on his side?"

My shoulders sagged. "No. I know that he had a brother in Egypt, but I don't know where he lives."

"Have you tried searching for him?"

"That's what I was doing at the café. I was trying to search forums."

His brows furrowed as he stared off into the horizon. "Maybe you'd have better luck with a private investigator."

I chuckled. "I can't afford that." I wished I could because it would certainly make my search a lot more efficient, but a PI was far too expensive.

He turned to face me. "What if your uncle isn't alive?"

My smile fell. My deepest fear gripped my body like a starving python. It *was* a possibility, even if I didn't want to admit it to myself. If my uncle weren't alive, it would mean my best chance of a connection to my dad, to all his childhood stories and history, would have died with his brother, too. And I couldn't accept that.

His eyes scanned my face. "I didn't mean to upset you."

I tried to shrug off the anxiety that squeezed my chest, but instead, my attempt at blinking back the tears produced the opposite result. Trails of liquid streamed down my cheeks.

Angry at myself for crying like a hot mess in front of my mentor, I swiped furiously at my tears, desperate to erase them from view. "God, I'm sorry for losing it like this.," I said, trying to chase away my embarrassment.

Dr. Campbell's large hand wrapped around my forearm. "Hey," he crooned, his deep voice coating my ears.

I cut him off before he could console me any further. "I feel so dumb right now."

But then he pulled me into his body, his arms surrounding me in a haze of warmth. I should have been startled by his action, but instead, his embrace lifted ten tons of weight off my shoulders. Weight that I had been carrying since the time I could process that my father would never be a family with Mom and me again.

More tears fell as I buried my face in his chest. I kept mumbling, "I'm so sorry," over and over again.

"Sanura, stop apologizing." Dr. Campbell's hand was rubbing large circles on my back. "I don't know what I touched on here, but I should be the one apologizing."

"I'm so stupid to have come here."

Dr. Campbell let out a soft chuckle. "You didn't have much of a choice. I dragged you here."

I shook my head, my forehead rubbing against the soft jersey material of his shirt. "That's not what I mean. I shouldn't have come to Egypt."

"Why not?" His hand moved slower against my back, giving me time to elaborate. Every so often, his fingers would tangle between loose strands of my curls, the soft tugging sensation registering at the base of my scalp.

I exhaled a huge puff of air before pulling back from his chest. His deep cobalt eyes studied mine as I mustered the courage to explain myself. "Part of the reason I came here was in hopes of reconnecting with my dad's family. It sounds silly saying it out loud, but I thought I could somehow reclaim my heritage through this internship. I grew up with just my mother, and even though she did her best to keep my heritage alive, I still never felt Egyptian enough."

I sniffled and my body shuddered, causing his hands to slide a little further down my back as he held me. He made no attempt to move them back higher, nor did I attempt to pull away from him completely. His touch grounded me. The man I had previously only known as a hard ass was enough to soothe me. It was bizarre, but I didn't dare question it.

"It's not silly," he assured me. "You grew up feeling lost, like a connection had been severed, and it's normal to try to regenerate it, just like your body would do if a nerve was severed."

I clutched at his shirt. "He has to be alive. I don't know how to explain it, but I just feel like he is." Maybe I was just desperate to kill this lonely feeling inside, but I truly believed my uncle was alive and that I would find him if I looked hard enough.

"He's alive. If you feel it in your heart, then he is."

Dr. Campbell cupped my face, using his thumbs to dry the remnants of my breakdown. His calloused touch held some sort of unearthly power that alleviated all my fears and worries.

I leaned into his touch, wanting to feel more of it. It was so wrong to be this close to my professor, but I didn't care. I was selfish, and I just wanted more of whatever this feeling was.

I couldn't shake his gaze. The comfort I had seen in his eyes just seconds ago had shifted into something darker. Hungrier.

All logic exited stage left as I lifted onto my toes and pressed my lips to his. At first, he remained still, as if still uncertain of my intentions. It was wrong and I should have pulled away, but I pled temporary insanity and parted my mouth slightly, catching a sliver of his bottom lip in a gentle nip between my teeth.

Like a time bomb just waiting to go off, he let me take advantage of his mouth. Seconds ticked by. Then he exploded into a fury of passion, fisting my hair at the base of my scalp as he devoured me. We moved against each other recklessly—me and my professor. This was fucking ludicrous but there was no way in hell I was stopping.

His tongue plunged into my mouth, hot and skillful, tasting every part of me. My nails dug into his chest like he was my lifeline.

Suddenly, he spun me around, slamming my back against the window. His solid body pressed into me so that I could feel every hard inch of him. I slid my hands underneath his shirt, feeling the ridges of his abs. The man was cut beneath his clothes, and I was dying to see it firsthand.

Our mouths moved together frantically, like we couldn't get enough of each other. Our lust enveloped us like a thick cloud against the cool glass, with all of Egypt below us to witness.

He broke our kiss, and I almost whimpered at the loss before his lips began to graze a trail down my neck. His teeth sank into the tender flesh there—just a little more pressure and he'd leave his mark on me for everyone to see. Marks that I wanted so badly to wear.

His stubble grazed my sensitive skin in the most delicious way.

Skillful hands palmed my tits over the fabric of my top. Clothes needed to go. His skin on mine was the only thing that could satisfy me.

I lifted my leg and wrapped my ankle around his lower back. My pussy ached with the need for friction, and I attempted to quell it by rubbing against his hardness. My eyes rolled back into my head from the thrilling sensation.

He dipped his head and bit my nipple. The sensation, even through my shirt and bra, caused me to cry out. The moan that echoed around me—my moan—sounded more feral than human to my ears.

"James," I breathed out, completely lost in him.

His body froze at the sound of my voice.

Awareness slammed back into me. Maybe I had been too presumptuous. I had never used his first name before, but it had rolled off my tongue as naturally as it felt to kiss him.

I tried again. "Dr. Campbell?"

But his name wasn't what bothered him.

He pulled away from me quickly. All sensuality had left his eyes, and instead, they were cold and hard, like stones.

"I-Is everything okay?" I stammered, my heart still racing from our tryst.

"You should go."

I searched his face for any hint of a joke or teasing but found none. "I d-don't understand."

"I'm your mentor, Sanura." His voice was stern. "I shouldn't have let this happen." He ran his fingers through his hair, my dusty pink lip gloss still slicked onto his lips.

"It's okay. You didn't take advantage of me. I wanted it, too." I tried to put my hand on his chest, but he pulled away before I could make contact.

He didn't even respect me enough to look me in the eye. "Please, leave. Let's just pretend this never happened."

And with those words, all the air was punched out of me. My cheeks heated in embarrassment. I had just had the best make-out session of my life, and the guy thought it was the biggest mistake of his.

Two options came to mind as I stared at him in disbelief: I could cry from humiliation, or I could slap his perfectly chiseled cheek.

I chose invisible option number three. "Fuck you," I spat.

I left the jerk standing there as I rushed away, grabbing my bag on the way out.

Chapter 12

"Let's just pretend this never happened."

"I poured my fucking heart out to him!" I whisper-yelled to myself as I dumped shards of pottery into a fabric basket. None of the rubble seemed to be of value since it had probably collected over time by way of voyagers flocking to the location, but I still had to be careful not to damage any of it. At most, the pottery would give us a better timeline of when the temple had been constructed and used. Anything found in the dirt would still need to be catalogued and recorded, but it first needed to be cleared out so that the team could dig through the sand that had contained it to find something bigger and better.

No one was in earshot of my bitching, and even if they had been, I probably wouldn't have stopped. Dr. Campbell was an asshole.

"Fucking dickwad," I seethed. *Dickwad* sounded so high school, but I wasn't in the mood to be mature about the situation. I was a woman scorned.

How the hell could he kiss me like that—*touch* me like that—and then just turn away like I was the biggest mistake he had ever made? It was insulting, not to mention humiliating.

Of course, I knew we had both crossed a line. This kind of thing would have been frowned upon in the States, but here in Egypt, it would be a moral scandal. Two unmarried foreigners grinding on each other wouldn't go over well with the conservatives at the Ministry of Antiquities. I couldn't even tell Angela about it because if anyone overheard, I'd be expelled from the program and Dr. Campbell would be fired—not that I truly gave a shit about what happened to him now. He could fall off a pyramid for all I cared.

He had made it clear that he wasn't concerned about my feelings this morning when I had arrived at the site. His reception of me had been icy; he hadn't even offered me a "good morning" like he had to the rest of the team. And now he was off under the tent enjoying afternoon tea and engaging in small talk with everyone like he was "Mentor of the Year." If that was how he treated the women whose mouths he shoved his tongue into, then so be it. I could be even *icier* than him and pretend it had never happened, too. Just put me in a slutty blue dress and call me *Queen Elsa*.

But God, his kiss! My lips still tingled from the memory. Never in my life had my mouth been assaulted that way. His taste. His touch. His rock-hard dick. Just thinking about it again almost melted away my newly adopted ice-queen exterior. *Almost.*

"Shit sucker," I muttered as I tossed more pottery into my basket.

"Am I interrupting?" Felipe's pleasant voice yanked me from my bubbling irritation.

I looked up at him to find the sun illuminating his head like a blinding halo. I used my hand as a shield and squinted my eyes. "Just talking to myself," I said, trying to play it cool.

"You call yourself a 'shit sucker' when you're alone? That sounds kind of emotionally abusive." He crouched down next to me, sorting clay pieces into my nearly full basket.

"I was singing a song." The lie sounded as stupid to my ears as it probably did to Felipe, judging by his raised brow, but it was all I could come up with.

Ever the gentleman, he went with it. "You'll have to teach me that song sometime. I'd love to hear it."

"Um...sure."

"How about over dinner? On Friday?" The corners of his eyes creased as he flashed another award-winning smile.

And my eyes...they bulged out of their sockets. "Wait, what? Like a date?"

"Well, sure. If that's what you want to call it." His expectant eyes made my stomach drop.

Felipe wanted to go on a date with me?

He brushed a lock of dark hair that had fallen across his forehead into place, his nerves beginning to show. "I understand if you are not interested."

My gut churned at having to turn him down. It made me feel so guilty because I should have liked him. He was so handsome with his dark features and bright complexion, kind of like that Disney Prince Eric with his pearly white teeth, white shirt, and fitted blue pants—or in this case, jeans. And his personality was so vibrant that it was impossible not to enjoy being with him.

Instead, I was hung up on the big oaf who was glaring at us from under the tent.

"I like you a lot," I started.

Felipe's forehead creased. "But...?"

My mind raced to find the right words. "But I'm just not looking to date right now." *Good save, Kitty!*

His smile dimmed slightly. "How about just going out as friends, then?"

My eyes darted again to the dirty-blond asshole who looked about ready to strangle innocent Felipe.

He had no right to show any interest in my social life, but the idea that I still affected him after his rejection gave me a high. Could the mighty James Campbell be jealous of his own student?

I knew it was wrong of me to do, but I wasn't above being petty. Not when I wanted to punish the asshole for pretending our kiss had never happened. Sanura "Kitty" Taha wasn't so easily forgotten by any man!

I donned my brightest smile, one I was sure Dr. Campbell could see from a mile away, and looked Felipe straight in the eye. I placed my hand on his toned forearm, the motion highly exaggerated for show. "I'd love to go out with you, *as friends.*"

If I were a mummy, then the god Osiris would surely cast my soul to damnation for this, but at least I'd have had the momentary satisfaction of getting under Dr. Campbell's skin.

Chapter 13

Ladies, always listen to your mother.

I should have listened when Mom nagged me to pack some nice outfits for my trip, because then I wouldn't have had to borrow another inappropriately sized outfit from Angela for tonight.

I kept one hand anchored to the hem of my dress so Felipe wouldn't get a prime view of my underwear as I climbed the narrow steps to the pub ahead of him. The peasant dress that she'd loaned me wasn't indecent, per se, but my ass was much larger than the firm nectarine Angela boasted. The hem kept rising higher than it should have because of my shape.

In America, it wouldn't have been an issue, but we were in a country where modest dress was preferred. Angela had convinced me that the length of the dress wouldn't be a problem when I had been getting dressed, and I had realized too late that movement, specifically walking, made it straddle the line of decency.

I climbed the steps quickly and reached the hostess booth in record time. Thankfully, my ankle was in fighting shape again. Felipe motioned to the hostess for a table for two, and we followed her to our seats through a bare-brick archway into the busy pub. Sounds immediately assaulted my ears. The loud chatter of patrons. The scrape of barstools against the cherry-wood floors. The voice of a commentator narrating a cricket game on the big-screen TV at the end of the room.

Most of the light was supplied by wall sconces littered about the walls. Photos of Buckingham Palace, Shakespeare, and other British memorabilia adorned the space. An oversized British flag that hung over the tchotchke-adorned bar transported me to a different country altogether. It was as if we had teleported to England by way of stairwell.

"This place is so cool!" I exclaimed as Felipe pulled a chair out for me. I eyed the bartender behind the counter serving a frothy glass of beer to another customer. "How are they able to serve alcohol here?" I had thought Egypt was a dry country, even though the ancient Egyptians had brewed their own beer and used it for temple offerings.

"Special permits," he replied, taking his own seat. "There are a few places around the city that cater to tourist locations, like hotels and restaurants. There's even a Mexican restaurant two streets down that serves margaritas."

My mouth watered thinking about spicy tacos with cold margaritas. "Oooh, I miss Mexican food!" The food in Egypt was delicious, but the Cali girl in me missed tacos.

"Let's take the rest of the crew there next time," he offered. "The drinking age is officially twenty-one and I think Isabella is the only one who is underage, though I don't think she'll be too keen on drinking anyway." His smile sparkled even in the low lighting around us.

I still felt guilty about accepting his offer to go out just to stick it to Dr. Campbell, but I didn't regret it. Felipe was easy to be around, and I enjoyed his company. It felt nice to be out with a friend and socializing like a normal human as opposed to the robots we were expected to be on-site.

I grinned. "That sounds like a great idea."

Just then, the waitress came to our table to take our order. Felipe ordered us a round of mild ale, and a plate of fish and chips for himself. I went with the cheese pizza because I was a basic bitch and there was nothing like beer and pizza on a night out.

I tucked a rogue bunch of curls behind my ear as the waitress collected our menus and left us alone.

"You look beautiful." Felipe's eyes scanned my loose tresses that seemed to have a life of their own tonight. No matter how much product I applied, my hair still looked like I had stuck my finger into an electrical socket with the dry air.

"Oh, thanks." I felt my cheeks heat. *Relax, Kitty. This isn't a date.* Felipe was a nice guy, and he was probably just paying me a platonic compliment. He was well aware that I was only interested in being friends, so perhaps it wouldn't hurt to return the sentiment. "You look great, too," I added.

He looked like a celebrity in his fitted crewneck T-shirt and jeans. His full head of dark hair was styled into a mock-messy do. I still swore he could pass as a famous soccer player or something.

"Thanks," he replied. "So, I have a question."

The waitress returned with our drinks and food. When she left, I said, "Shoot."

"How come you go by 'Kitty' and not Sanura?" he asked, dunking a fry into the tiny cup of ketchup.

I took a long chug of my first alcoholic beverage in weeks, letting the heady taste roll over my tongue. "It's not that I hate the name. I think I just grew tired of having to explain how to pronounce it all the time. Growing up, my teachers would have a hard time getting it right, so I got fed up and just went by Kitty because it was foolproof to pronounce."

I held up a slice of my gooey pizza to offer to him.

"No, thanks.

I took a bite. It definitely wasn't as good as a pizzeria pie, but the orgy of chewy dough, melted cheese, and tomato sauce hit the spot. "Good, because I don't think I want to share it with you now."

He chuckled before returning to the topic. "Well, I guess you're finally in a country where everyone can pronounce your birth name. By the way, did I pronounce it correctly?"

"Perfectly!"

He picked up another "chip." "Thank God for the way Dr. Campbell enunciates your name, like he's pissed at you or something. It made it easier for me to learn it."

I smiled awkwardly. The mere mention of Dr. Campbell's name was enough to make me grimace. Every time my name rolled off his tongue, it sounded like a curse. Like a dirty secret he wanted no part of.

"Speak of the devil." Felipe nodded over my shoulder.

My scalp prickled before I even turned in my chair.

Dr. James Fucking Campbell.

He was the picture of casualness as he leaned back in his chair. The dark button-down that he wore fit him like a glove, highlighting his broad chest and thick arms. Those deep lines that I'd believed had been permanently etched onto his forehead at birth were gone. Instead, he donned a careless smile, the kind that a person wore when they were with someone they genuinely enjoyed—the kind that I had never had the privilege of witnessing.

He wasn't alone, either. A woman with long, dark hair, smooth like her perfect fair skin and glossy like onyx, sat across from him. The delicate fingers of her right hand propped her chin up, displaying her firecracker-red nails as she seemed fixated on his every word. Even though their table was at the far end of the T-shaped room, the blueness of her eyes glimmered across the distance to taunt me.

She seemed older than Dr. Campbell, maybe by ten years or so, but looked like one of those famous socialites you would see in *Vogue* who held lavish balls only open to the elite.

"What is *he* doing here?" I huffed out, turning back to Felipe.

Felipe lifted his beer glass in Dr. Campbell's direction before taking a swig. "Looks like he's on a hot date."

Blood bubbled under my skin. This wasn't part of the plan. Dr. Campbell was only supposed to think Felipe and I were getting closer, not have a front-row view of our night out, let alone enjoy a romantic night out of his own with the prettiest woman in town! This was even more embarrassing than his rejection post-window-humping! *Ugh!*

I glanced back at him again. Maybe he wouldn't notice us. I mean, he was tucked away in the corner with his eyes glued to the gorgeous creature in front of him. He wouldn't have to pass by us to leave the pub. At least I could preserve a bit of my dignity.

I turned around just in time for the waitress to check on us.

My hand went to my still nearly full glass, and I tipped the entire contents down my throat in four large gulps. Felipe and the waitress gaped at me as I slammed my empty glass down onto the table. "I'll take another."

***

Three beers and lots of undercover spying later, I was teetering on the wire between tipsy and *downright drunkity drunk.*

I tried to focus on the words that were spilling out of Felipe's mouth, something about stealing his dad's car...or uncle's car...or neighbor's car...*someone's* car. It was probably a funny story, but all I could think about were the two love birds behind me.

Just a week ago, Dr. James Campbell, archaeologist extraordinaire, had been two seconds away from fucking me against a window for the entire town to see, and here he was on a date with a goddamn model. I bet he hadn't even given me a second thought when he picked her up tonight. She'd probably wrapped her legs around his hips to greet him as soon as she opened the door. She seemed like the type...like a daddy longlegs ready to sink her fangs into him.

And now, they were all cozy together, talking as if they were reciting the entire Merriam-Webster dictionary, when Dr. Campbell had always seemed like he was conserving his word count with me. What did Miss Pretty Face have that I didn't that made him so interested? There was no way she could have looks to kill *and* a winning personality. God just didn't work that way. You got one or the other. It was against the law of the land to have both!

Who was I kidding, getting jealous over a woman this mature? I was a student whose life involved eating pasta shaped like farm animals out of a can while pulling all-nighters just to learn half as much as Dr. Campbell knew. He fit better with a woman like her.

"Kitty?"

I swung back around rather clumsily to find Felipe—a rather blurry version of Felipe that wouldn't stop swaying—staring expectantly at me with the waitress at his side.

"Huh?" I croaked.

His forehead creased. "I asked if you wanted to order anything else before I paid the check."

My teeth were on full display in as earnest of a smile as I could muster. "Oh...no, thank you."

I felt horrible that I'd ignored Felipe for most of dinner. He had been so kind to take me out and pay for my meal even when it wasn't meant to be a date.

"Are you okay, Kitty? You seem a little...distracted." His concern made me feel even worse.

I waved him off. "I'm fine. I think the beers went to my head, is all." I hadn't drunk like this in a while, and I was already a lightweight with alcohol. The beers were definitely clouding my judgment, and testing my bladder. "I do need to use the restroom before we head out."

"Sure." Felipe stood up as I left the table, like a true gentleman. Guilt gnawed at my conscience as I walked in the opposite direction of Dr. Campbell's table to the bathrooms.

My bladder was much happier after I drained it, though. Too bad it wasn't the only thing that was drained. A deeply frustrated woman stared back at me in the mirror over the sink. This wasn't me, the type of person to blatantly ignore a friend or to obsess over a guy who clearly didn't want me. I needed to get a hold of myself.

I turned the faucet on and worked the crystal-blue hand soap into a silky lather between my palms. After rinsing them off, I reached for a paper towel and held it under the stream of water.

Moving my mass of untamable hair from my neck, I pressed the cloth to my skin. The cool water revived me, bringing me back to my senses.

One step at a time, Kitty.

First thing's first. I was going to walk out there and apologize to Felipe for my inattention. It was the least I could do after ruining the perfect night out that he had planned for us.

Then, we would leave the pub without casting another glance over at Dr. Campbell and his floozy, if they were even still around.

I could do this.

The wet paper towel catapulted into the trash can and I made my way out the door and into the long corridor that led back to the dining area and bar.

My carefully crafted itinerary for the rest of the night also flew into the trash when I registered the looming figure leaning against the wall just outside the restrooms.

I gasped. "Dr. Campbell? What are you doing out here?"

He said nothing. His hooded eyes raked over my body, lingering on my thighs.

I scoffed at his audacity. How dare he ogle me while his girlfriend or whoever was out there waiting for him? *The nerve of men!* They want to have their triple-layer fudge cake and to scarf it down too. "Triple-fudge" out there could have him.

"Shouldn't you be with your *date*?" My tone came out snarkier than I had intended, but I didn't give a fuck.

But he didn't answer. Instead, he moved in closer, caging me between his hard chest and the wall. His hypnotic scent—old books and whiskey— enveloped me. "That boy isn't right for you," he growled.

Unbelievable! First, *he* wasn't right for me, and now, Felipe wasn't either. This guy was a royal pain in the ass.

"You don't know what's right for me." His face was so close to mine that anyone could walk by and clearly witness our dangerous entanglement. We'd be arrested for indecency.

I pushed against him, but he didn't budge. "Go back to your date, *James*." I used his name pointedly, hoping to knock some sense back into him. It had proved to be an effective cockblocker last time.

The sinister smile that rolled onto his lips proved me wrong. "Say it again." *His name.*

I refused to give him that satisfaction. "Miss Longlegs out there looks like she has no problem saying your name, just like you have no problem listening to her every word."

"You were watching us?" His smiled widened at my deep scowl.

I bit my lip, already feeling guilty that I had just given away my secret, toxic obsession of the night. *Time to find a new one.*

"You're jealous," he hummed, like the idea pleased him.

I turned my head to avoid having to look at his smug expression a minute longer, but his fingers gripped my chin and pulled me back. "She's not my date, Sanura." My name rolled off his tongue like a sinner begging for mercy. "She's my colleague."

"Do you always wine and dine your colleagues in dark corners of pubs?" I spat.

My venom failed to break his shield. "Stop it," he commanded.

I would never relent. "Leave me alone."

His eyes pierced mine, even in the dark hallway. "You are the only fucking woman I think about."

This guy is really something else with these rehearsed lines. "And you're a liar."

"Then explain why I can't stop looking at you whenever you're around."

His hand slipped under the hem of my dress, leaving a trail of goosebumps up my thigh. My breath quickened with every inch that he traveled.

He dipped his head low and whispered so close I could feel his breath on my lips, "Explain why images of you play in my head when I'm alone, like a movie, robbing me of any peace."

Immediately, he spun me around, pressing my chest to the wall. His front blanketed me, his turgid length pressing into my back. "Explain why my dick gets hard every time I see your face."

I could hear the distant chatter from the bar. "Someone could see us," I whispered, but what little fight I had left was slowly slipping away.

"I don't care." His warm breath caressed my ear. His hand played at the waist of my panties. "Tell me to stop again, Sanura." It was a dare—a dare that I was powerless to take.

Instead, I backed my ass up into his warm body, inviting him to explore. His fingers plunged into my panties, finding my wetness. My body was a traitor for loving the fight.

"Your body isn't as stubborn as you are." He found my clit and began working it in tight circles.

My knees shook as my professor fingered me in public. It was so dangerous. So forbidden.

"More," I begged under my breath. Later, I would launch a detailed analysis into why I'd caved so easily, but right now, *more* was all my lust-filled brain could comprehend.

"This pretty little cunt is mine. All. Mine." The possession in his voice gripped my chest like a vise.

I hid my smile against the hard wall. *I wasn't the only one who was jealous.*

His fingers moved faster, winding me up toward impending release.

God, nothing had ever felt so good in my life. I moaned against his touch as my nails scraped against the flaking paint of the wall.

A palm immediately covered my mouth, silencing me, as he plunged two fingers into my eager slit. He must have been hunched over because I felt his dick against my ass. I ground against him.

"Fuck," he panted in my ear. "You're going to make me come if you keep moving like that."

I teased him some more, his arousal spurring me on, and I rolled my hips faster. I wasn't going down alone.

Hearing his breaths turn ragged behind me only heightened the sensation of his fingers fucking me. His hold loosened around my mouth, and I caught his middle finger with my mouth, sucking it like I yearned to do to his cock.

"Shit," he cursed.

I rolled my tongue around the tip of his finger, wishing I were teasing his head. My hips bucked when I felt another digit slide into me. I was so close. I knew he could feel it, too, from how hard my pussy clamped around him. His thumb pressed against my clit, offering a final blow.

"Kitty?"

I gasped at Felipe's voice at the end of the corridor. The warmth I had felt around me—*in me*—instantly disappeared.

I turned my head quickly to search for Felipe, but luckily, I couldn't see him. He must have still been just beyond the hall, too far to see me.

I spun around to face James. He could never go back to being "Dr. Campbell" after what we had just done.

"I'm coming," I called out, hoping to buy myself a moment to adjust my dress so I didn't look like I had just been finger-banged in a dark hallway.

James winced as he adjusted the hard ridge in his pants, then he shot me a final possessive glance. "You. Are. Mine," he mouthed, before storming off to the men's restroom.

I collapsed against the wall, catching my breath as the sound of Felipe's footsteps approached.

Chapter 14

"Kitty, you're a fucking liar," Angela huffed as we trekked up the steep hill.

Bikes whizzed by, cars honked, and people cluttered the roads as we walked, all moving at a faster pace than the two American girls trying to find their way.

I looked around to see if anyone had overheard her foul mouth, but no one seemed to have noticed amongst the chaos.

"Felipe is so hot, and you expect me to believe that your date only involved beer and pizza?"

"It wasn't a date!" I protested. I didn't know how many times I'd have to remind her of that before it sank into her slightly undersized head. On anyone else, a cranium so small would have made them look like a baby bird, but it worked on Angela—gave her a dainty quality that men apparently loved.

She rolled her eyes so hard that I swore they were in danger of sticking. "Again, you're stupid for not making it one. Or, you could have at least tapped a sister in if you didn't want him for yourself."

"He's all yours if you want him."

She shot me a quizzical look. "You seriously don't find him sexy?"

Felipe was really good looking, but the attraction just wasn't there. "I don't."

"You must be blind, because there's just no other explanation for it." Her sentences were littered with pants for breath as we walked. The roads weren't smooth, and our lungs—not to mention our calves—were paying for it. Thankfully, my ankle could handle the stress, and my feet continued pounding the pavement, determined to get to our destination. Angela, the goat-yoga enthusiast, did a poor job at keeping up.

"Felipe said Dr. Campbell was there, too," she huffed.

I halted in my tracks. My hands clenched in irritation. "You spoke to Felipe about our night out?" She was supposed to be my friend. I'd have to check the bylines again, but I was pretty sure talking about me behind my back violated girl code.

"Relax! We weren't gossiping or anything. I woke up to pee in the middle of the night and ran into Felipe on his way out of the bathroom. All I asked him was how his evening was, and he offered up that Dr. Campbell was on a date with some good-looking chick."

It had been irrational of me to jump down Angela's throat like that, but that's what James did to me. He turned me into a paranoid maniac, and I couldn't shake this nervous feeling now that I had heard his name.

"Did Felipe say anything else about me?" He hadn't seemed suspicious of me lurking in the corridor at the pub. I'd covered for my flustered appearance by saying that I wasn't feeling well, and we had left for the hostel soon after.

Angela grabbed my elbow, and I paused to glance at her. She was red-faced, blonde hair sticking to the sweat on her neck. "Why are you being so paranoid?"

I shrugged her hand off. "I just don't like being talked about."

"We weren't talking about you! He didn't even utter your name. Jesus Christ, you need to get a grip." Her loud voice attracted unwanted attention from curious pedestrians.

"Sorry," I muttered as I continued walking, wishing I could take back my outburst.

But Angela stayed rooted to the spot. "Are you hiding something?"

"What?! No!" I shot back, the tips of my ears suddenly hot. If she busted out some red robes and a cross, confessional-style, I was leaving her ass on these streets. "Why do you say that?"

"You just seem so defensive."

Guilt gripped my stomach. Aside from my mom, Angela was the only person I shared my secrets with. However, *this* secret was one that I couldn't share with anyone.

I sighed. "I'm just exhausted." This was partially true. We had taken an early flight out of Luxor to Cairo. It was only an hour's worth of air time, but we'd had to leave first thing in the morning if we wanted to make it back to the airport in time for the last flight back to Luxor in the evening.

Thankfully, Angela decided to drop the subject of my suspicion and continued walking. "So, how did Dr. Campbell's date look?"

Another jaw-clenching topic.

"Fine," I gritted out.

Angela must not have noticed my tone. "*Fine*?! That's all you have to say? No details?!"

She was really pissing me off with her questions. I should have come on this trip alone.

"Uh...I don't know. She was pretty." She was more than fucking pretty; she was a damn supermodel. James had said that she was just a colleague, but could I believe him? I barely knew him—although, yeah, his fingers had been knuckles-deep in my vagina, so it was safe to assume that we were at least on a first-name basis now.

"I can't imagine him on a date," Angela said. "He's so serious all the time. I bet you he's a man who just fucks you raw and leaves you wanting more."

My heart started racing like it was going to burst in my chest. "Not me. I'm not fucking anyone," I answered hastily.

Wrinkles formed on her nose. "I didn't mean *you*, Perfect Polly. I know you're not fucking anyone. After your failed date with Felipe, I'm starting to believe that you're asexual."

I threw my hands in the air. "It wasn't a date!"

"Yes, yes. We all know about your *non-date*. Calm down! So, what was Dr. Campbell wearing?" Her eyebrow hiked with renewed interest. The woman was incorrigible when it came to the topic of men.

"Why are you so interested in him?" It bothered me that she kept bringing Dr. Campbell up.

"I need some new material for my bedtime masturbation."

My hands flew to my ears. "Ewww! Please, stop!" I shared a room with Angela, and I didn't want to know what she did under her covers while I tried to sleep barely two feet away.

She scoffed. "You're such a prude. You know what your problem is?"

"No, but I'm sure you'll tell me."

"You need to be bent over and have something thick rammed up that ass instead of the stick that's been wedged inside it for forever." She smacked my backside playfully.

I grabbed my ass and looked around, mortified that she had just done that on the streets of Cairo. "Angela!"

"What?" She giggled at my horror. "You need some softening up."

She wasn't exactly wrong. I was on edge. How could I not be with the unfinished business of what I endured at the hands of *our* mentor? Only a moment longer and who knew what James and I would have done. We could have been caught and arrested for indecency. I would surely have been let go from the internship program, and James would have been fired. There was too much at stake for something that was too unclear between us.

What were we? Even though I had hated him for pushing me away at his penthouse, I couldn't deny our attraction. And it had relieved me to find out that he felt it too. He had said that I was on his mind all the time, but even so, I had no clue where I stood with him. The only way to find out was by having a serious conversation, and *talking* and *James Campbell* never went together.

I couldn't risk telling Angela for fear of snooping ears. What if someone overheard us and reported it to the ministry? She clearly had no volume control today, judging from all the eyes that were on us, so what made me think she could keep quiet about something this big?

"How much longer until we get there?" she groaned.

I pulled out the scrap piece of paper from my bag and examined the address scrawled on it. "I think it's the next street over."

We turned the corner and continued our journey.

"What if the address is wrong?" she asked.

It was a risk I was willing to take. I would evaluate any lead I came across to find my uncle.

Imagine my surprise when I'd received a response to one of my many forum posts asking about my uncle's whereabouts. User "mmmefoodie465" had replied saying that their parents had been friends with a Yusuf Taha from

Cairo. I had sent a private message to mmmefoodie465 asking to confirm other relatives of Yusuf Taha, and they had mentioned my father's name. My heart had galloped when they'd given me the last known address of Yusuf Taha and his wife.

I hadn't hesitated to book the next available flight out to Cairo. Driving would have taken us at least eight hours, not counting bathroom and food breaks, so flying had seemed more practical.

"This is it." I stopped in front of a run-down building that looked more like a haunted dwelling than a home.

"Are you sure someone lives here?" Angela scrunched her nose again, this time at the dingey brown stains on the once-white paint. The windows of the two-story house had a yellow tinge, and the iron gate in front of the door had rusted over time.

The hope that had ignited within me after receiving the message with information was slowly dimming the longer we stood in front of the house.

I pulled at the gate, and it swung open with a loud screech. The door behind it was ajar as well.

"I don't think we should go in there. It doesn't look safe."

But I ignored Angela's concern. Perhaps my uncle and his wife lived a modest—very modest—life, and I wasn't going to judge them by the appearance of their home.

I pushed the door in and stepped inside.

Dust swirled around us, and the dank smell of mold and ammonia made me cover my nose with my bicep.

Angela coughed into her sleeve from the rank scents that encircled us.

Meowww.

Cats. More cats than I could count on one hand sauntered up to us. I could place the acerbic scent now. *Cat piss.*

"I don't think anyone lives here," Angela wheezed.

My eyes scanned the dark area, looking for evidence of more than just feline life. No furniture remained in the house. The ceiling looked to be about one thunderstorm away from caving in, based on the missing patches I could see.

The house was dark and empty, much like how I felt inside. Perhaps James was right. Maybe my uncle was no longer alive. All I had left were the ghosts of my family to haunt me for the rest of my life.

My eyes fogged up with tears, more from emotion than the scent that engulfed me.

I had only been a child when my father passed away and couldn't even remember the day he died. My whole life, I had longed for the presence of a man I didn't really even know. But in this moment, I felt like I was mourning him for the first time. Like he had just died, and the wounds of his loss were fresh in my heart.

A sob escaped my throat as the pain finally caused my tears to spill over.

"Oh, Kit." Angela wrapped her arms around me and held me as I cried into her shoulder.

I had been stupid to believe in this fairytale of finding my long-lost uncle for so long—the last connection to my father. James was right. I shouldn't live behind rose-colored glasses anymore. Living life with that much hope only led to disappointment because there was nowhere to go but down.

Chapter 15

Campus was bustling today. It was unheard of to spend dig days away from the site since the excavation season was so short, but we were required to attend today's lecture. James had arranged for our internship team to attend and left Mo in charge of the dig team at the site for the day. The lecture was going to be filmed for *National Geographic* and would feature an anthropologist from Louisiana State University, Dr. Blossom Moore.

I had never had the privilege of listening to any of her lectures, nor did I even know what she looked like, but I knew she was famous in the anthropology community for her work on mystic religions.

"Hurry up. We're going to be late," Isabella barked over her shoulder.

Sean's face twisted as he checked his watch. "We're like five minutes early!" he said as we filed into the packed auditorium.

"*Fifteen* minutes early is actually *on time*. Five minutes early is LATE." Isabella shoved through the lines of people waiting to find a free seat and plopped herself in one of the reserved seats in front of the stage, leaving us behind.

"She's fucking nuts," Sean huffed.

Beside me, Angela hummed her agreement and said, "I'm not sitting next to her."

Yeah—no, thanks. "Me either."

"Let's sit over here." Sean pointed to four free seats off to the side of the stage. It was out of the field of view of the cameras, so no one would see us on film. And there weren't any other seats directly behind ours since the side rows were all staggered.

"Where's Felipe?" Angela looked around.

"Restroom," I said. "Maybe we should save this end seat for him so he can just slide in, since we're late and all," I teased, pointing to the seat on my right.

"Good idea," Sean said, taking his seat on the other side of me.

"Who wants to bet that Isabella asks questions during the taping?" Angela snarked.

We all chuckled as the lights in the auditorium flickered, signaling the beginning of the lecture.

My eyes roamed the hall. There must have been hundreds of people in attendance. Students. Professors. Researchers. It was so exciting to be in such a diverse room. I hoped there would be time after the taping to mingle so I could meet some of the viewers.

Three large cameras were stationed about the hall, aimed at the brightly lit lectern on the stage. People scurried around, checking the lighting, testing mics, doing whatever it was *National Geographic* film crews did.

Scanning the audience, I found the man who I'd known would be there. And he looked like a fucking snack in his three-piece charcoal suit. I had never seen James so dressed up, and I couldn't pry my eyes away. It wasn't just the outfit, it was him. He wore clothes like it was his own skin, with the confidence of a god. His hands rested in his pockets as he stood strong and tall, deep in conversation.

Then he leaned over, getting closer to the person who held his attention.

That woman. He had called her a colleague, but I only knew her as his date.

She was seated before him, her long legs crossed under a black pencil skirt, and her attention was focused solely on James. Her silky hair was wrapped into a French twist—who even wore that style anymore?—just above her neck.

James rested a hand on the armrest next to her as she whispered into his ear.

I hadn't seen him since the night at the pub, and I felt jealousy simmering just like it had that night.

Suddenly, his eyes caught mine, and he flashed me a smirk as he stayed hunched over his *colleague.* He reminded me of a mischievous teenager with a secret.

The lights cut out in the auditorium then, leaving only those that shone upfront on.

James stepped onto the stage. He lightly ran his hands over the smooth wood of the lectern.

A woman dressed in all black, who I assumed was part of the film crew, signaled to him from below to speak.

With the ease of an experienced orator, he began. "Ladies and gentlemen, thank you for being here today. I have the distinct privilege of introducing our guest speaker. A pioneer in the field of anthropology, Dr. Moore has revolutionized the study of mysticism as it pertains to history. As a professor from Louisiana State University, Dr. Moore introduced the field of

Mystic Studies with an emphasis on the spiritual world. Through her re-search of spirit possession and spells, she has brought to light the intangible as it relates to the physical world, allowing us a deeper understanding of our ancestors and their beliefs. Her work has earned her the prestigious Margaret Mead Award."

His deep voice was steady and calm as he glanced around the hall. The audience hung on his every word, and even though it was in English, every-one seemed to comprehend what he was saying.

"Now, without further delay, welcome my good friend and brilliant col-league, Dr. Blossom Moore."

Applause broke out as a woman stepped forward—

Holy shit! James's date was Dr. Moore?

She walked to the center of the stage with the grace of a gazelle. She took both of James's hands in hers, shaking them softly, before trading places with him behind the lectern.

Damn...I realized he had been telling the truth. She really was a col-league.

Dr. Moore began speaking, but my eyes stayed glued to James. His body moved swiftly around the side of the stage. Instead of taking Dr. Moore's va-cant seat, he kept walking—*walking toward me.*

My eyes widened in shock when he sat down next to me. My fixation only greeted me with a smug smile, which he quickly concealed with his fin-gers hooked over his mouth. I looked to my left to see if anyone had noticed, but my friends seemed to be captivated by Dr. Moore's lecture.

Straightening in my seat, I decided to follow their lead and focus on the slides that Dr. Moore was presenting on spells used during the mummifica-tion process. *Look at the pretty picture of the decaying mummy. Ignore the sound of breathing from the sex god next to you. Don't think about his fingers fucking you into oblivion in dark hallways.*

Too late.

My cheeks heated at the steamy memories that filled my head, and I re-adjusted my posture to quell the tingling between my legs.

Someone shifted too, simultaneously opening his legs wider to brush against mine.

Immediately, my eyes darted to the side. Sean was completely absorbed in the lecture. Angela wasn't waggling her brows at me. No one seemed to have noticed a thing. Thank God the auditorium was dark. The last thing I needed was for an audience focused on me rather than on Dr. Moore.

His leg remained pressed against mine, daring me to pull away. Well, two could play at this game.

With my attention trained on the stage, I re-crossed my legs, angling them toward his seat. My knees pressed against his thigh. If anyone glanced at us, it would just look like we were sitting in a cramped space.

Peripherally, I could see his smile spreading wider behind his fingers. He dropped his hands and clasped them on his thighs, casually resting his elbows on both arm rests.

My turn. I slid my hands smoothly between my thighs, sandwiching them like I was cold. My elbow flared out to invade his space, resting on the shared armrest between us with mine touching his.

At first, he remained still, as if unaffected by my move, but then he leaned his head slightly toward me. "Be careful," he whispered, his breath hot on my skin.

Satisfaction bloomed inside of me. I had cracked his stoic exterior. It was a dangerous game we were playing for anyone to see, and I was winning.

"You started it," I replied, keeping my voice low.

Suddenly, he pressed his leg harder against mine, making full contact with my shin. The faintest gasp escaped me, and I bit my lips to keep them shut.

My mind raced to come up with my next move. I couldn't let him have the upper hand. If he wanted to be risky in public, then I would show him just how daring I could be.

I freed my hands from between my thighs and pulled on the elastic band holding my ponytail in place. Black curls rained down my back. I raked my fingers along my scalp, shaking them out to their fullest volume. Without warning, I tossed the mass of ribbon-like waves over my shoulder, brushing him with the strands. Suavely, I rested my chin on my fingertips, using the arm rest for my elbow.

I sat there trying to bite back the smile that threatened to overtake my lips as my hair draped over his arm. Now he'd have to sit through the rest of the lecture with tendrils sprawled over him. Served him right for starting this little game with me.

But my smirk disappeared when I felt a slight pull at the ends. The slow, winding motion made the base of my scalp prickle with sensation. My eyelids lowered as I savored the feeling and envisioned him wrapping my locks around his fingers. The blanket of curls must have concealed his hand from view. Slowly and rhythmically, the tugging moved about the base of my head. As any girl with a full head of long hair could tell you, it felt so damn good.

I blinked my eyes open in case Sean chanced a glance at me, but it was too hard to focus on Dr. Moore, who was moving animatedly across the stage, probably sharing some interesting fact that I should commit to memory.

Instead, I was in a haze of bliss. His hands worked a new section of curls, and the winding and pulling sensations sent my eyes rolling back in my head. It wasn't long before he had my core vibrating with need.

He continued his torment, and all I could think about was having his fingers pulling on my hair while I rode him hard. I should have felt guilty or embarrassed for the dirty thoughts in my head, but I didn't give a fuck.

My head tipped backward subtly, offering him more of my hair. I bit my lip, trying to fight back the moans he was invoking. My hand fell to my lap and my nails dug into the fabric of my skirt. Pants of exhilaration shook my chest.

Suddenly, the sound of applause broke out, startling me from my pleasure-filled flirtation. The presentation was done. My hands immediately mimicked those around me, even James's, which were no longer snaked into my hair. I stared at him as he clapped from his seat, but his face gave away none of the secretive things we had just done in the dark.

About to rise from his seat, he whispered gruffly, "Go to my office." It wasn't a request, it was a command.

And just like that, he morphed into Dr. Campbell, proud and always appropriate, as he strode to the stage to shake hands with Dr. Moore.

I slumped back in my seat to recover from the tornado that had just plowed through my body—the tornado named James Campbell.

Chapter 16

"What an interesting lecture!" Isabella gushed as she scanned the notes she had recorded in her notebook for completeness.

"It really was fascinating," Angela chimed in. "I'm hoping we get a chance to introduce ourselves to Dr. Moore. She seems like such a powerhouse. Her research was so eye-opening."

"It was good, but I personally would like to meet with her to point out a few findings she forgot to include," Isabella said.

I rolled my eyes. *Typical.* Perfect Isabella schooling everyone, including world-renowned researchers.

Felipe joined our circle outside of the auditorium as masses of students and professors filed out of the doors. "Hey, guys."

Angela patted his shoulder. "Where have you been? We had a seat for you."

"I couldn't find the auditorium, and by the time I did, the lights were already off, and filming had started." His eyes flashed to me. It was quick, but

I noticed something in them that I couldn't quite place. "I saw Dr. Campbell join your row, and all of the other seats were taken, so I stood in the back."

Crap. Did he see anything?

"You stood for the whole lecture?" Angela asked in disbelief.

My palms grew sweaty as I studied his face, praying that my suspicions were wrong.

"Yeah. It was no big deal. Dr. Moore was interesting enough to distract me from the leg cramps," he teased. His expression seemed too casual to have noticed Dr. Campbell and me.

Sean nudged my shoulder. "You seemed to be really into her presentation."

"Huh?" I gaped at him. *Was he looking at us, too? Shit!*

"I looked over at you and your eyes were shut like you were entranced or something."

The cackle that broke through my lips startled the group, and even myself. "Yeah, you know. I was just trying to absorb every word." My excuse was shit, but everyone seemed to buy it.

I was thankful to Felipe for changing the subject. "Should we head over to the dining hall? I think that's where everyone is mingling."

Sean clutched his stomach. "Yeah! I hope they have something to eat. I'm starving!"

"Let's go!" As usual, Isabella strode off first, while the rest of the group followed behind.

All except me. I stayed rooted to the spot.

Angela turned back to me. "You coming, Kitty?"

James had asked me—no, *commanded* me—to come to his office, and to be honest, I was still so drunk off his antics during the lecture that I wanted to obey.

"I—um—need to use the restroom," I fibbed.

"Well, don't take all day. I saw some hot guys in the hall, and they looked like they're just begging to be jumped." She waggled her brows excitedly.

"Angela!"

Her only response was a wink before catching up with the group.

***

The faculty floor was silent except for the echo of my flats on the polished floors. It had taken me a moment to find my way since the archaeology building was massive. Three flights of stairs that my ankle didn't enjoy later, and with a slightly sore ass, I found myself wandering through a maze of doors and dark wood molding.

Dr. James Campbell.

His name was etched in gold font over the glossy black plaque on the wall adjacent to the lucky door.

My fist hesitated.

What was I doing? He had ordered me here and I had just obeyed like it was second nature. I was losing all sense when it came to him, but I still couldn't walk away. Curiosity was too strong for me to ignore. The excitement of seeing how far I could go without getting caught had consumed me.

I knocked softly and waited. And then again, slightly louder this time, but that went unanswered, too.

Looking around to see if the coast was clear, I pushed the door open and stepped inside.

"Dr. Campbell?" I called out, using his professional name in case anyone overheard, but the room was just as I had suspected. *Empty.*

I closed the door behind me and took in his environment. It looked to be a standard office, nothing spectacular, with a desk, swivel chair, and two guest seats in front—all made of the same dark wood that adorned the university hallways. The chairs were neatly arranged around the desk, which was meticulously organized, typical of what I would expect of its Type A owner. Behind the desk was a panel of windows that would probably have cast welcome sunlight into the dated office if the blinds had been open.

His space. Though it was most likely bare because this wasn't his home university, the office was still infused with his presence. His scent perfumed the air around me—a warning that I was in his territory. I was at his mercy in this room.

My eyes scanned the wall of books adjacent to the windows. I meandered closer, my fingers grazing the spines. Books of all bindings filled the shelves, from glossy textbooks to fabric-bound compendiums. The shelves were deep enough to house two rows of books, one in front of the other, if he ever needed more space for his collection.

It would be lovely to have an office and book collection like this to call my own one day. Years from now, I hoped to have achieved *something* in the field; I would be happy with even half as much success as James.

Without warning, the door swung open, and all the breath left my lungs. James rushed inside, twisting the lock with his fingers before turning to me. His body was taut like it was a locked vault of pent-up energy.

Slowly, he inched toward me, stalking me like prey.

My back hit the shelves as I retreated from his hungry gaze. "James?"

But he didn't reply as he closed in on me.

Hard ridges of wood dug into my back. Adrenaline made it hard to think clearly. "I think Felipe might have seen something."

"I don't care," he growled.

He should have. His career would be on the line if anyone were ever to see us—to see this.

His tall frame towered over me, caging me in like a caught rabbit. *The big bad wolf with eyes that shine so bright. The better to see me with.*

Those deep blues trailed the length of my body. His fingertips skimmed the skin of my vibrating chest, down to the valley between my breasts, concealed just beneath my shirt.

"You're a bad girl, Sanura," he hummed. "Teasing me like that in a room full of my colleagues. The cameras could have filmed you."

As if it were no obstacle at all, he slipped the top button of my shirt through its hole, exposing more of me to his hungry gaze.

I tipped my head back, hypnotized by his full lips.

"Do you like other people watching? Does that get you off?"

"If I say yes, will you still want to pretend this never happened?" I shot back, hitting him with his dreadful words from the past.

Instead, his lips twitched into a half smile. "So confident that something is going to happen before it's even started, eh?"

"Maybe it's because I know you better than you think," I whispered.

Another button slipped open, exposing the black cotton cups of my bra. *Damn, I wish I had packed cuter underwear for this trip.*

"What do you *know*, my precious Sanura?"

My cheeks heated at the endearment.

I angled my chin high, looking him square in the eye and willing my voice to remain steady. "I know that you like the chase. It's a game to you, and after you've had your fill, you'll move onto the next thrill that passes your way."

"You don't know shit," he spat, causing me to flinch. He leaned in closer, his breath warm on my face. "Because I could never have my fill of you."

His lips crashed into mine, devouring me like I was his last meal. The world around us seemed to mute as our hands groped each other and tongues intertwined in a mad rush. My shirt flew to the ground. His jacket was shoved off his shoulders.

The scruff on his chin scratched my neck as his he tasted me. He tugged my bra down roughly, revealing my breasts to his pleasure. Though they felt heavy from lust, his large palms engulfed them, making them seem even smaller than they already were.

He groaned as his eyes feasted on what his hands were doing. "Your tits are so perfect with these pretty dark brown nipples." His tongue swirled around one peak, sending my back arching. Wood dug into my shoulders, but I didn't give a shit, not when James was making me feel so damn good.

I had always felt self-conscious about my body. My skin wasn't quite as tan as my father's, nor was it as light as my mother's. It was a shade somewhere in between that still allowed me to sport the tawny freckles that sprinkled my skin from sun exposure. My nipples apparently took after my melanated heritage—dark brown on my olive skin. They had always felt mismatched to me, but with the way James was worshipping my breasts, I felt like Hathor—the goddess of beauty and love.

I nearly convulsed on the spot when his teeth nipped my sensitive peaks.

"You like that, baby?" His words floated over my skin.

My fingers clenched at his scalp, urging him to continue. Strong, wet licks worked my bud over before he moved onto the other one.

His tongue trailed down my belly, dipping into my belly button. There was no doubt he could feel my core quaking from his touch.

"James," I moaned.

I watched as he flashed me a wicked smile, the kind that sent liquid heat pooling in my panties.

"So forthright, calling your professor by his first name." He hooked his fingers in the elastic waist of my skirt as he positioned himself on both knees. "You're a bad student who needs to be taught a lesson. Maybe my hand across your ass would teach you some respect."

His smirk just edged me on further. "You're a bad teacher," I groaned out. "Taking advantage of your student like this."

But he was too smart and caught me on a technicality. "I believe you signed a waiver to be in my care for the duration of your internship."

I scoffed. "Is that what you're calling this? *Care?*"

"Care doesn't always have to be gentle. Do you want me to show you what I mean?"

I nodded, my heaving breath robbing me of my ability to speak.

He pulled down my skirt, tugging when the waistband caught as it passed over my ample ass. The fabric fluttered to my feet before he pushed it aside to free my legs.

He traced the V cloaked in cotton between my legs. "This looks almost too pretty for me to corrupt. I bet what's underneath is even prettier. Will you let me see, Sanura? Will you let me see your pretty pussy, my kitten?"

Feelings inside of me warred with each other. He was my mentor, and my brain kept flashing red lights, warning me that this was wrong and that the consequences weren't worth it. But my body felt like it would die if he didn't make me his.

My body won. "You're my mentor. Mentor me." I pushed my hips forward, begging him to proceed.

Without hesitation, he ripped my panties down so fast that my ass jiggled in response.

The tip of his nose caressed the stretch of hair that covered my most intimate parts. My legs instinctively drew together to hide their apex.

Grooming hadn't been a priority during this internship, and God, was I suddenly mortified!

"No," he commanded, separating my thighs. He tickled my clit with the tip of his tongue, and my knees buckled on contact. He liked me...all of me.

He picked up his pace, stroking me fast with his tongue.

I tipped my head back, savoring the sensation, and let my whimpers and moans vibrate out of my throat freely. It felt so good, I couldn't care. My shoulders rested on the edge of the shelf, and I raised my arms overhead and gripped one a level higher for support. I parted my legs a little wider to give him more access, all inhibitions leaving my body. "That feels so fucking good."

His hands moved to my ass, gripping the flesh like he was holding on for dear life. The intensity of his touch was almost too much to bear, yet too addictive to halt.

I lifted my leg over his shoulder. His head dove into the extra space I had created, lapping at my slit. "Mmm," he thrummed against my sensitive area, sending a shudder through my body. "You taste delicious. Like warm vanilla."

The idea of how I tasted had always made me cringe for some reason, but hearing it from his lips was like an aphrodisiac. I wanted him to drink me dry.

He continued his assault on my pussy, as one of his hands drifted up toward my breast. His fingers twisted my nipple. The twinge of pain set me off, the urge to orgasm rushing through me. I rocked my pelvis against his face, needing more friction to get there.

"Put your other leg around my head."

I obliged, draping it over his free shoulder. His hands gripped my ribcage under my breasts as he carried me across the room. I clutched his hair as he moved us like I weighed less than a feather.

He planted my ass on the smooth desktop. I pulled him toward me, pressing my mouth to his. Kissing him was by far my most favorite thing in the world—well, after having him eat me out.

I could taste myself on him, and he wasn't lying. It tasted like a sweet and musky drink, and it didn't turn me off one bit. Instead, it ignited my fire knowing that I had infiltrated his mouth, leaving my presence there.

Our tongues clashed in a messy wrestling match. I clawed at his waist-coat, struggling to undo the buttons, but his hands stopped me.

"I want to see you," I whined.

"And I'm not done tasting you. Bend over my desk."

I couldn't argue with that. He was masterful with his tongue, and if he wanted to continue honing his skills on me, then so be it.

I planted my feet on the floor and leaned over the desk. I felt his fingers massage the base of my scalp. Then they slid down my spine, bathing me in sensation from his callouses. There was no mistaking that a man was touching me. Both of his hands squeezed my fleshy ass, pinching the fullness before him.

"The things I want to do to this ass, my kitten." *Slap.* The sting from his palm seared my behind.

"So full and thick, just begging to be tamed." *Slap.* I cried out as my fingertips dug into the hard wood.

Suddenly, he shoved my lower back down, forcing my torso onto the desk. My cheek lay flat, leaving me unable to see anything behind me.

I felt James spread my cheeks. I gasped when something wet swiped over my slit and up to my hole.

"Your hole is so tight, and tempting me to fill it," he groaned.

My knees shook. "I'm not ready," I panted out. I'd never done anal before, and to be honest, I was scared. I had heard stories of it being painful.

But his voice was unhurried. "Don't worry, kitten. I won't take you there today, but one day soon."

Soon? Did that mean there would be more of this? No more of him regretting anything before it even started?

I felt his tongue bury itself in my warm slit, working waves of pleasure through my channel. His nails dug into my skin, piercing my flesh like blades. It should have hurt, but I was too far gone to register it as anything negative. I was discovering that I had a thing for pain.

His attention slid to my clit where he rubbed circles against me with his fingers, edging me nearer to release. I could feel myself dangling over the precipice.

A knock at the door was like a bucket of cold water over my euphoric blaze.

"James?" a heavily accented, muffled male voice said from the hall.

"Fuck," James grunted as he straightened up. I scrambled to adjust my bra, but he pushed me back to the desk. Panic pulsed through my veins.

The knock blared again, and the doorknob squeaked as it twisted. Thankfully it was locked. "James, you in there? They need you for photos." The man must have been a colleague, too, if he was calling James by his first name.

I heard the faint release of James's zipper. "I'll be out in a moment, Riaz. Just need to take care of some business first." I felt the tip of his rigid dick at my pussy. *Oh, God.* He was going to fuck me while that man was on the other side of the door.

Instead of slamming into me, the tip of his cock beat against my lips. Repetitive thumps against my sensitive skin. The speed at which he worked himself hit all the right spots. I bit my lip to keep from moaning aloud.

"Okay, I'll meet you in the lunch hall," Riaz said through the door.

"Be there soon," James called out, his hoarse voice nearly giving away his depraved behavior.

Footsteps faded away into the distance and James picked up his pace, beating himself off at warp speed against my sex.

"Aren't you scared we'll get caught?" I bit out as the erratic pumping pounded against me.

"Nothing can keep me away from this ass right now." His free hand slapped my cheeks again, jolting me forward on the table. "If you don't come, I'll have no choice but to fuck this pretty hole that you don't want me to touch."

His threat pushed me over. The image of him slamming into me from behind sent me crying out in ecstasy. "Oh, God!" Stars glittered behind my eyes, and all I could hear was blood rushing in my ears. My knees nearly gave out from under me.

Suddenly, I heard the strangled grunt of the man behind me. "Jesus." Sounded like I wasn't the only one who had just seen God.

Before I could catch my breath, I felt liquid warmth jet onto my ass— wet and sliding down my thigh.

His forceful pants evened out as his hand smoothed comforting circles on my back.

The sound of his zipper ripped me from my hormone-induced high. Something soft swiped at the cum that had forged a river down my leg. The sticky residue remained as I carefully straightened up, the stiffness in my shoulders and back from our stunts finally registering.

When I turned around, I found James fully dressed, as if our tryst had never happened. Not a wrinkle in his jacket nor a hair out of place. I felt so awkward with him dressed up while I was nearly naked. Then his fingers grasped my chin and tipped my face up to meet his warm gaze. Where there had once been lust and contempt, something else had shifted into view—something softer that made my chest bloom.

He extracted a small square of paper from his jacket pocket and handed it to me. "Call this number."

My brow hitched and I stared from the paper to him expectantly, needing more of an explanation. But all he did was press a soft kiss to my lips before walking out the door.

I leaned heavily against the desk, my legs shaking like Jell-O—and unfolded the note.

Aaqil Bukhari

095-555-5555

Chapter 17

The folded square of paper burned a hole in my pocket.

I couldn't wait to get back to the hostel and investigate the number that James had given me. After a quick shower to wash off the smell of sex, I threw on my bright blue pajama set dotted with flying llamas.

I sat cross-legged on my bed with my wet hair frizzing out from lack of care. It would look like a rat's nest tomorrow from the lack of product, but I didn't give a shit. Curiosity wrung my belly into knots.

A quick Google search revealed the identity of the mystery man on the paper. Aaqil Bukhari, Private Investigator of the Greater Cairo Area.

A PI? My mind raced with a bunch of shady conspiracies. Maybe James was involved in bounty hunting or some shit and wanted me to join his side hustle? Or maybe he was a secret assassin who worked with this investigator...like a two-for-one deal for anyone looking to *off* a person?

Whatever the reason, I had to call the number to find out. I wouldn't be able to sleep until I did.

The line rang twice before it was answered with a quick, "Hello," followed by, "*Assalamu Alaikum*," which meant, "Peace be upon you."

I returned the greeting. "*Walaikum salam*. My name is Kitty—I mean, Sanura Taha, and I was given your number by a *friend*, James Campbell." I wasn't so sure we could call ourselves friends, but this stranger didn't need a dissertation on the complexities of our relationship.

"Ah, yes. Miss Sanura," he replied in English. "Give me a moment to pull up your file."

My file? Why would this guy have a file on me? "Look, I'm not sure why—"

He cut me off. "Just a moment." His tone sounded like he wasn't too fond of bullshit, so I opted to stay quiet.

I overheard the tapping of computer keys as I waited for him to be ready.

Suddenly, he cleared his voice. "I have found it. The search for Yusuf Taha."

I nearly dropped the phone when I heard my uncle's name.

"Um, yes." *How did he know my uncle's name?*

"After gathering your demographic information from James, I was able to piece together past whereabouts of your uncle."

"I see." The words choked my throat on the way out. I was utterly stunned at what James had done. I recalled sharing my wishes to find my family at his apartment, but I hadn't expected him to do anything about it.

I supposed James could have used the required information from my internship application, like my father's name and date of birth. But why would he have gone through all that trouble on my behalf? "After graduating from the University of Cairo with his degree in business, Yusuf Taha appears to have married a woman by the name of Miriam Salah. She is the daughter of a successful textile manufacturer."

"My aunt," I breathed out. This was wild. My uncle had a wife—a family! "Did they have any children?" I blurted out in excitement.

"Two. A boy named Shiraz, and a girl named Shireen."

My heart was racing so fast that my head felt dizzy. "Are they still alive?"

I held my breath, feeling the familiar ache of the disappointment I had felt when I'd visited the abandoned house in Cairo pierce my chest.

"It would seem so as I haven't found any death records with their names listed."

This was too good to be true. My insides bubbled with excitement. "Where are they?"

"That, I don't know yet. They lived in Cairo after they married for nearly twenty years before relocating. I have no leads yet on their whereabouts.

Thoughts raced in my head, making it difficult to articulate. "Do you think you can find them?"

"I'll need some more time."

"How much longer?" I was desperate to find them soon. What if we waited too long and something happened to them, like a freak accident where I would never get to see or even speak with them?

"I'm not sure. But trust me that I'm working as hard as I can."

Hope. That was all I'd had my whole life, and I just needed to hang onto it a little longer.

The idea of payment crossed my mind. This must cost a fortune, and I didn't know if I had enough to cover his fees. "Um...I'm not sure what the going rate for your services is, but I'm kind of on a budget."

"Unnecessary," he answered bluntly.

"I'm sorry?"

"My fees have been taken care of, so no need to worry about payment."

James. My eyes burned with the liquid that pooled in them.

"Can you call me if you receive any updates?" I could barely speak, so overcome with the tears that clouded my eyes.

"I'll definitely do that."

I swallowed the lump in my throat. "Do you need my number?"

"Already have it."

Of course, he did—he was a PI with a caller ID.

"Do you have any more questions for me, Miss Sanura?"

I couldn't think anymore. My heart was squeezing too tightly for me to think logically. "No, thank you."

"Then you have a good evening. Goodbye."

"Bye." The line went dead.

I gripped the phone in my shaking hand.

There was only one place I wanted to be right now, and it wasn't my bed.

Chapter 18

I pounded on the door. It was late as fuck, but I didn't care.

It had taken a lot of fast talking to convince the concierge to allow me upstairs. I'd had to drop the "distraught intern" card, lying through my teeth that I desperately needed to speak with my mentor about my fake dissertation, before the balding man in an ill-fitting suit would allow me to take the elevators up to the top floor. I supposed the tears streaming down my face and llama pajamas had been enough to convince him, or at least get me the hell out of the ritzy lobby without causing more of a scene.

The wait was killing me. I banged on the door again.

The lock clicked from inside, and then the door swung open, revealing a drowsy James.

His shirtless torso, sweatpants, and bare feet only confirmed that he had been asleep, when here I was, storming his floor like a banshee. Surely, Mr. Cranky Concierge had paid him a quick phone call to alert him that a crazed woman was throwing a fit to see him, so my presence wasn't a complete surprise.

"Sanura? What are you doing here? It's midnight, and we have to meet at the site at five." He ran his fingers through his mussed blond hair. "How did you get here from the hostel?"

But I couldn't speak.

His eyes must have gained some focus because they went wide when they caught sight of my tears. His hand grasped my elbow. "Kitten, what's wrong?"

I launched myself into his arms, my lips crashing into his. The taste of my salty tears mixed with the peppermint of his toothpaste as my tongue sought refuge in his mouth. We stumbled into the penthouse and the heavy door shut on its own.

My fingers glided down the hard grooves of his pecs and abs. Hard like perfectly chiseled stone, even at rest. The desperate need to be close to him fueled my kisses. But the mere stroke of our tongues wasn't enough to satisfy me. I pulled at the waistband of his pants frantically, yearning to feel all of him against me, on top of me, and inside of me.

"Wait." He gripped my shoulders, stopping me from undressing him. "Tell me why you're crying. Is it because of the PI? Did he have bad news?"

No. Only good news. Everything was right.

How could I begin to explain how I felt? This man in front of me was so mercurial and confusing. Never would I have expected him to do something so selfless for me like paying for a PI.

"I just need you," I pleaded. I didn't want to talk, I just wanted to feel. I wanted to show him my gratitude.

I toed off my flats and kicked them aside. My hands worked the buttons of my baggy pajama top, releasing each one quickly before James tried to stop me again. As I'd hoped, his eyes remained transfixed on my breasts. Next, I slid my pants and panties down my legs and stepped out of them.

The vein in his neck pulsed as his heavy-lidded gaze raked over my bare body in the dim light of the living area. I was desperate as fuck to be under him, but now that I was naked, I felt self-conscious. I fiddled with my frizzy mess of hair, bringing it forward to cover any part of me it could to keep from being so exposed.

"Don't do that."

"Do what?"

"Don't hide yourself from me. I need to commit every inch of you to memory."

I had a hard time accepting that a beautiful man like James could worship my body like it was gold. "Why me?"

He pulled on a tendril of my hair and coiled it around his fingers as if it were smooth as silk. "I should be asking you the same thing."

My forehead creased with confusion. He could have had any woman he wanted. He was gorgeous, brilliant, and successful, a literal wet dream for any lucky lady out there. But here he was, eyes hungry just for me. No man had ever looked at me the way he did, turning my core into molten heat with one glance.

The pad of his index finger pressed against the sensitive flesh in the valley of my tits, burning me on contact. "Your light shines so bright, and God help me for wanting to bathe in every inch of it."

My heart doubled in size at his words, and the yearning I had felt when I walked through his door morphed into something deeper.

I dropped to my knees before him. His breath hitched as I tugged on his sweatpants, revealing his length. My gaze locked on inch upon inch of rigid steel and my mouth watered for a taste. His cock was just like the rest of him, a work of art—hard yet magnificent.

I swiped my tongue over my lips, wetting them in preparation. I had done this a number of times before, but somehow, this time felt like the first, like I was a blow-job virgin.

I could feel his eyes scorching my skin from above.

The bead of precum threatening to drip from the tip was enough for me to give into temptation. My tongue swiped over the smooth head, the salty silkiness tickling my taste buds. His low groan rumbled through my core.

Sealing my mouth around the tip, I sucked on it like it was the first taste of a fresh popsicle in the summer heat. And just like a popsicle, he melted in my mouth.

"Fuck," James breathed out. He fisted the hair at my scalp hard.

The intensity of his reaction spurred me on. I flattened my tongue to make room for his length and started to move. My fingers dug into his hips, holding on as he rocked them closer to me, feeding me his length. His thick shaft jerked in my mouth as I worked him in and out, hitting the deepest reaches of my throat.

Lucky for both of us, my threshold for gagging was pretty high.

"Kitten, how the fuck are you able to take all of it?" Amazement cracked through his haze of lust. "I can feel you so deep, and it only makes me want to hurt you more."

I was amazed that I could take nearly all of him, minus about two inches, and even still, I was determined to make it fit. It was a challenge that I wanted to conquer. *Put it on my sexual resumé. Notarize it. Laminate it.*

I slipped one of my hands down to his balls, cupping and massaging them as he fucked my mouth. The flavor of him permeated my mucosa, dominating my senses of taste and smell.

"Oh, fuck." His moan echoed in my ears. Nothing else beyond him existed right now. It was just us, in this moment.

His shaft grew inside of me and I felt like he was close. I was obsessed with the idea of his cum in my mouth, dripping from my lips.

I dragged my finger behind his balls, applying pressure on the thin flesh.

"Woah." He cupped my chin, nudging my attention to his face with his dick half-stuffed in my mouth. "I won't survive if you continue."

That was kind of the point.

"Stand up. I want inside of your pussy. Now!" he ordered.

I reluctantly obeyed, already mourning the taste of him.

He stepped out of his pants, then in one swoop, he threw me over his shoulder like a ragdoll. I yelped in surprise as he stalked through the living room and up the stairs with me inverted.

"I don't even want to begin to imagine how you became so good at giving head," he murmured, tension tightening his tone.

I giggled at his irritation. "Practice." Though I had only had a handful of sexual encounters that had resulted in intercourse, I did have enough experience with blow jobs, which had apparently worked in my favor tonight.

His palm landed against my bare ass, stinging my plump flesh. "Knock it off. I'm the only one who gets to mark this body from now on, understand?"

I stilled. Did this mean that he wanted to be exclusive?

We traveled the rest of the way through his massive home in silence until he threw me onto a bed like a caveman tossing his latest hunt onto the ground.

His bedroom was just as chic as downstairs, with a high black paneled ceiling and stainless-steel hanging light fixtures over the dark bedside tables. His bed was way more plush than mine at the hostel was, and his storm-gray sheets were softer than anything I'd ever felt, even though they were already rumpled around my body.

He prowled up my body to seal his lips over mine. His kisses were addictive—heat mixed with meaning. His tongue wrestled with mine, making me lose all consciousness of time and reality.

His hard cock pressed against my belly as the sounds of our hungry kisses and frantic breathing played like the chorus of a song.

I couldn't help the moan that escaped me when he ran his tongue down my neck to my tits. His mouth caught hold of my nipple, sucking it between his teeth. His sharp little bites sent pulses of pleasure shooting down my body to my dripping pussy, and I wove my fingers into his disheveled hair, pressing him harder against me.

Those romance books had been right: hooking up with your professor was hot as hell!

"Oh, God. Fuck me now, Dr. Campbell," I cried out, the words flying out of my mouth without a thought.

He froze on top of me, and I silently cursed myself for the accidental role play. But then his mouth fixed into a sly smirk—he had enjoyed it. "My little intern likes it when I bite her pretty nipples?"

I licked my lips. The way he played along with this little fantasy made me tingle with excitement. I nodded, pressing my thighs into his hips and wishing I could rub myself against him.

He plucked my other nipple with his mouth, gently tugging before releasing it.

"What else does my intern like? I want to make sure your time with me is worthwhile."

"I like you *down there,* Professor." I played coy, jutting my chin down toward my pussy, even though only moments ago I had begged him to fuck me.

"Are you asking for an oral exam, Miss Taha?" he hummed, his eyes glistening with mischief.

My fingers played at the scruff on his chin. "If that's what my professor thinks is in my best interest, then yes."

"Then, I wouldn't want to disappoint a future archaeologist."

He slid down my body and positioned himself between my legs, groaning in appreciation of what he saw. "This cunt! So wet and ready for me. You're fucking perfect."

I sucked in a sharp breath. His praise always had that effect on me. "Oh, please. I know you just want a five-star review on ratemyprofessors-dot-com."

"I don't even know what that is, but don't make me punish you for that smart mouth."

"You say it like it's a bad thing. Just think of me as quick-witted."

"Whatever it is, I know how to shut you up before you ruin your grade."

Before I could respond with another witty comeback, his tongue drew circles on my clit. "Ah," was all that came out of my mouth.

"That's more like it. Kitty and her pretty pussy that tastes like honey. So addictive and sweet."

His tongue swiped at my soaked slit, and my toes curled from the sensation. "Jesus."

My hips rocked, pressing my swollen lips into his face. His stubble pricked my sensitive skin, heightening my sensation.

He pulled away and sat back on his heels. His lips were slick with my arousal. "I need inside of you now."

I was ready and eagerly parted my legs wider for him.

"Condom first." He was about to climb off the bed when I stopped him.

"I want to feel you. I'm on birth control." Most women on digs were on contraception, to make their periods more predictable or to prevent them altogether.

"Here I am, trying to be responsible, and then you go and say things like that." He lined up his head with my entrance, and I could feel his warm velvet tip touch my sensitive flesh. "I'm clean," he grunted, the sensation clearly affecting him too.

"Me, too," I breathed out in anticipation.

Without further delay, he slammed into me. All hints of playfulness had completely vanished.

"Fuck, you're so tight."

"Maybe you're just too big," I ground out. His size was crammed into my hole like when I tricked myself into thinking that my ass could fit into a size-small bikini—tight as fuck.

"Your mouth is only going to make it bigger, kitten." He pounded his dick into me, hitting the top of my vagina with each pass.

I clenched at the sheets beneath me, needing anything to ground me during his welcome assault.

His breath grew ragged as he drilled into me. The line between pain and pleasure blurred into a delicious mix of confusion, just like our relationship. The headboard banged against the wall as we fucked like primal beings.

I felt myself clamp down around him, signaling my impending release. "I'm close," I said, panting.

James grabbed my leg and rested my foot on his shoulder, opening me up more for him. The feeling intensified as he filled me in a way that I had never felt before. I cried out from the rawness. It was all too much, but I didn't want it to stop.

His pants turned into sharp grunts.

A scream left my throat as a sweet orgasm ripped through my body. James followed me into bliss, roaring his release as his hot cum filled me.

He continued pumping into me as we rode the waves of ecstasy together.

Then, suddenly, he blanketed my body with his, propping himself on his forearms so as not to crush me. His breath tickled my neck as we lay together, the sound of our thumping hearts evening out.

When our sex high wore off, he pulled out of me. I grieved the loss, feeling empty and hollow without him inside. He ventured through a door, which I guessed was a bathroom, because moments later he came back with a washcloth and set to cleaning me up. Thoughtful, yet too intimate.

After cleaning himself up and discarding the cloth, he lay down next to me. I curled into his side, swinging my leg over his body.

"Now, do you want to tell me what all of that was about?" he asked, resting his hand on mine on his chest.

"Thank you." It was all I could say.

He knew what I was referring to. "I take it that you called the number?"

"My uncle's alive. He has kids." I could feel the tears returning, happy ones.

"Where are they?"

"I don't know. Aaqil says he needs more time."

He squeezed my hand. "He'll find them."

"How can you be so sure?"

"Just a feeling."

"You didn't have to pay him."

"I'm sure it's frowned upon to not pay a PI for his services," he teased.

"No, I mean that you didn't have to do that for me."

He didn't reply. It seemed he wasn't very good at accepting gratitude.

I lifted onto my arm and pressed a kiss to his lips, ready to thank him in ways that I knew he would accept.

But he threw a bucket of cold water on my plan. "As much as I want to fuck you until daylight comes, you need to get some sleep. We have a long day tomorrow and need to be up in two hours."

I wanted to stay with him tonight, even if just to catch a few hours of sleep by his side, though I wasn't sure he was inviting me to stay. The team would have a million questions for me if I didn't get back to the hostel before they woke up. Angela would strangle me until I spilled every detail.

"I should get back before anyone talks."

"I'll drive you home." I could sense the reluctance in his body language. Maybe he did want me to stay after all.

I bit back a giddy grin. "Thanks."

Chapter 19

I had reached the hostel just in time to throw my sheets over my body and shut my eyes tight before Angela's alarm blared across the room.

That was a close one.

I did my best impression of a woman who'd gotten a full night's rest when inside, I was exhausted as hell. I only had the memory of last night's delicious sex to keep me motivated throughout the workday. Sneaking glances of Dr. Sex God in between disguised yawns would have to serve as the hit of adrenaline I'd need to stay awake.

My act must have been convincing because Angela hadn't said a word all through breakfast, or on the shuttle ride over to the site. *The Academy Award for Best Performance by a Sexually Hungry Intern goes to Sanura Taha.*

I stepped out of the shuttle and was immediately blasted by the hot, dry air. It was already hot as hell, even though the morning sun had yet to fully break through the dim sky.

The rest of the workers had already arrived and were busy preparing the tools needed for the day.

I scanned the grounds to find the pair of blue eyes I hoped would be searching for me, too. His tall figure emerged from the temple with a flashlight in hand, followed by a visibly flustered Mo and another man whom I didn't recognize. The stranger looked important, dressed in a white polo shirt and tan slacks with a clipboard in hand. A gold badge that hung around his neck glowed in the distance.

James switched off the flashlight and pelted it onto the dirt in front of him. I watched as the other man spoke a slew of words, his expression unimpressed. The wrinkles that had already settled on James's forehead for the day deepened. He flicked open the buttons of his sleeves and roughly rolled the fabric up to his elbows and then crossed his arms over his chest. He was pissed.

Mo stood between James and the stranger with his hands on his hips, his sweaty face bouncing between the two men like he were watching a table tennis match.

"Who do you think that is?" I asked Angela.

Instead of answering, she pulled on my arm, dragging me away from the rest of the team. "Where the fuck were you last night?"

Fuck. I supposed my acting *hadn't* been good enough to fool her.

When in doubt: deny, deny, deny.

"I have no idea what you're talking about. I was asleep right next to you, you stoned sleeper."

She scoffed. "Don't twist this on me and my love for sleep. Your text was bullshit. 'Going to the store for tampons. Don't wait up'?! Bitch, we're on the same damn birth control cycle and not due for Aunt Flo until a month after our return flight! If I hadn't passed out from exhaustion soon after my shower, I would have notified the army over your lame ass story!"

I grimaced. I knew the text I had hastily sent her before rushing over to James's place had been poorly executed, but I'd been in a hurry and needed anything to keep her quiet for the time being. I should have spent more than two seconds thinking up an excuse.

"The Egyptian army? You'd call the Egyptian army because I wasn't in our room? Isn't that a bit dramatic?"

She wasn't buying my attempt at de-escalating her overreaction. "Where were you, Sanura Taha?!"

I was suddenly aware of how dry my mouth felt as my eyes darted over to James, who was still preoccupied with his guest. The irrational hope that he'd look over at me and save me from Angela's interrogation twisted in my chest like a screw. Now would be a great time for him to shout for me to help with a menial task like sorting his pens by color.

"Shut up!" Angela exclaimed.

My eyes flashed back to her. "What? I didn't say anything."

But she was staring where, or rather at whom, I had been looking moments ago.

I froze, my eyes wide. *Shit.* I shook my head and waved my hands frantically in front of her to keep her quiet, but it didn't work.

Words spewed out. Hands flailed in the air. "You?! And *him*?! When? How? What?!"

I grabbed her wrists and gripped them tightly. "Shhh! I'll answer all your questions, but please, keep it down!"

She pressed her lips together, her cheeks puffing out like she was ready to vomit more incoherent words at any moment.

"You cannot ever repeat any of this! Swear to me on your last-season Gucci boots."

Her eyes grew two times larger above her puffy cheeks. "The ones with the gold double-G buckle and quilted strap?!"

"Swear to me, damn it!" I whisper-yelled in her face.

She exhaled the air she had been holding in, sending my hair flying around my face. "I swear on the House of Gucci." She was ever the fashionista, and ever the Lady Gaga fan.

I took a deep breath before starting, wishing I could take five more and down a shot of tequila, too. "Yes."

Angela let out a gasp but then quickly covered her mouth with her hands after catching my severe glare.

"It just happened and I don't know what it means, but you can't say anything. Pretend this conversation never existed."

"Fuck," she breathed out. "You and our professor?! What the hell?! What if he gets in trouble? No, wait, what if *you* get in trouble?" She pressed a hand to her heart. "Oh, fuck, I'm going to have to bail you out of Egyptian jail just like your mom warned. But this time for being loose!"

"I'm not loose!" I protested.

"I know that, but the ministry won't see it that way!"

"You need to calm down. You're going to draw too much attention to us!"

"How did this happen?"

"One day, I was at his place—"

"You were at his place?! Since when do you know where he lives? God, I barely know you anymore, Kitty!"

I rolled my eyes. "If you want to hear the details, then pause the dramatics for a second!"

"Fine. At least tell me something good. Is he good in bed?"

I couldn't hide my satisfaction. "The best."

"Fuck me!" she exhaled.

I smirked. "My words exactly."

She smacked my arm. "You're making jokes while I'm freaking out from the biggest news I've heard since Britney was emancipated!" The girl loved her some Britney Spears, too. "Free Britney" had been in her Instagram bio for nearly a month up until the star's release.

"I wanted to tell you, but I wasn't sure if there was even a thing to tell." James and I hadn't discussed what was happening between us. Each sexual encounter could have been the last time we ever fooled around, as far as I had been concerned.

"Are you two in a relationship?"

"I don't know." My shoulders sagged. Everything suddenly started to feel real. What future did we have, anyway? I was still a student in America, and he was a professor in England. We would be miles apart, and he was a man who already had an established career.

"I see." I knew what she was thinking—that he was just some man in a position of power getting his rocks off.

"It's not like that," I argued.

"I didn't say anything."

"Yeah, but I know that you're thinking he's just a professor taking advantage of a student. It's not like that."

"Then what's it like? Help me understand."

"I don't know, but when we're together, it feels like nothing I've experienced before. Like the passion is so strong that I can't see beyond us."

She sighed. "Shit, Kitty."

"What?"

"You're in love."

"What?! No!" Certainly not. We were just two consenting adults who had great chemistry and enjoyed eating each other out. *God, why did I have to go there?* My panties weren't durable enough for how turned on the man made me.

A wicked smile spread over Angela's face. "I've never heard you talk about a guy like this."

She was full of shit. We'd never even been out on a date! There was no way I was in love with him.

Right?!

I had to put an end to this dangerous line of thought. "Look, it's just a summer fling. That's all."

"Whatever you say," she mocked.

"Just promise me you won't say anything." The last thing I needed was any of this getting to the wrong ears—then, it would surely be over between us.

She nudged me with her shoulder. "Who am I going to tell? Isabella?"

I looked over at our resident Ms. Know-It-All, who was instructing a group of workers about something that they probably already knew. Bitch probably had a direct line to the police chief programmed into her phone for situations like this.

"I won't tell anyone," Angela said. "Just promise me you'll be careful." She put her arm around my shoulders.

"I promise."

"Less talk, more work!" Mo had sneaked up behind us, clearly in a shitty mood.

"We were just discussing our dig strategy for the day." Angela gave me an exaggerated wink. *Smooth, girl. Smooth.*

His cheeks flared out like an angry puffer fish. "The minister is here breathing down our necks, and you two are out here cackling. Are you looking to have our grant revoked?"

The stranger speaking to James was from the ministry? No wonder everyone seemed so tense.

"They want to revoke the grant for the dig?" I asked in disbelief. We still had three more weeks left.

"If we don't have any developments soon, yes. They will not renew the project."

"What about the bracelet I found?" That had to have been something more than just a piece of jewelry.

Mo wiped his sweaty brow. "The report isn't back on it yet, so as of now, we technically have nothing."

Angela and I stood there, stunned at the news. The temple had only been unearthed last year, and it was clear that there was a story behind its construction. We still hadn't figured out who had commissioned it. It surely hadn't been a pharaoh.

I looked over at James, who seemed to be in a heated discussion with the minister under the tent.

"Wow, that's shocking," Angela said, shaking her head.

"Do yourself a favor and at least look busy so Dr. Campbell doesn't take his frustration out on you," Mo warned. This was the nicest he had been to us during the entire dig—saving our necks from James.

Angela and I parted ways, feeling the pressure of the situation on our shoulders. I joined Abdul just beyond the back wall of the temple. He smiled at me and handed me a hand shovel and brush.

I stooped down next to him and went to work.

Thirty minutes and a basket full of broken pottery later, the minister was still at the site hovering around. James's fuse had grown increasingly short, his temper threatening everyone in his path. I was lucky to have been spared so far, but I knew it was only a matter of time before he unleashed his wrath on me. The man could dish out fury just about as good as he could dish out dick.

I dug my shovel into the sand again, and the metal clanked against something. Abdul looked over and swiped his brush over the area. Dark blue and red paint on stone peeked out at me. It almost looked like a child's toy. I brushed away the sediment until I could free it from the sand.

A statue. It was small, about the size of my index finger. I held it in my palm, the heavy weight indicating that it was made of solid material and not hollow inside.

The face had been chipped away, but the figure had a headdress that pharaohs wore.

I read the cartouche at the base of the figure. "Ay." Tutankhamun's successor.

Why was his statue here at a temple devoted to Tutankhamun, especially when Ay was believed to have forcefully secured the throne after the young pharaoh's death? Ay had even used Tutankhamun's original tomb for himself, forcing the dead king to be buried in a small, uneventful tomb, the very same one that Howard Carter famously excavated in the 1920s.

Abdul shouted for James. The minister came trotting along behind him.

"What is it?" James asked as he kneeled next to us, finally making eye contact with me for the first time today.

His masculine scent reminded me of our night together, fully enveloped in his smell, his arms, and his kisses.

I shook the naughty thoughts from my head. "A statue." I placed it in James's palm, trying to ignore my fingers making contact with his skin and liquid heat racing up my arm in response.

He studied it for some time, with the minister peering over his shoulder.

James's finger brushed over the cartouche.

"Ay," I read aloud for the men.

"What is he doing here?" the minister asked loudly, referring to the figurine.

James's eyes locked with mine. The satisfied smile that spread over his lips was a sight to be seen. He directed his words to the minister: "Convincing you to renew our grant."

Chapter 20

Two pharaohs at one site?

The riddle stumped me as I poured over peer-reviewed articles on my laptop in one of the study rooms at the university. It was my day off, and I should have been out with the rest of the crew sightseeing, but I was determined to figure out why the figurine of Ay was at a temple built for Tutankhamun.

My over-worked eyes scanned the pages of the various New Kingdom textbooks strewn about the table, hoping the answer would pop out at me, but my mind remained blank. I took another bite of the granola bar that I had brought along for brain fuel, and the crunch of dried oats and nuts filled my ears.

"Ahem."

My mouth halted mid-chew as my eyes tracked the source of the interruption. James was leaning against the doorway with his arms crossed over his chest and an amused smile on his lips.

I swallowed the still-too-big chunks of granola, the jagged edges scraping my throat on the way down. "Hey," I said awkwardly, reaching for my bottle of water.

"Hey," he replied, not awkwardly. But really, was the man ever awkward? His constant confidence was unnerving. I guessed researchers of his caliber had God-complexes that worked in their favor.

"I didn't know you'd be here today," I replied, straightening my chaotic work area.

"Just stopped by to sign some documents," he said casually.

"Oh."

His eyes raked over my appearance. "Cute look."

I patted the messy bun at the top of my head, held in place by a full pack of bobby pins and the two stray pencils that I had been searching for fifteen minutes ago.

I hadn't had any alone time with him since our night at his place, and as result, I felt extra flustered with all of his attention on me now.

I narrowed my eyes at him. "Since when do you use the word 'cute'?"

"Trying to expand my vocabulary."

The corner of my mouth lifted into a crooked smile.

He pushed off the frame and closed the door behind him. "Why are you here?" His fingers twisted the wand, closing the blinds over the windows to the room.

I rubbed at my eyes, which were tired from all the blue light I had exposed them to over the past three hours. "Trying to figure out why that statue of Ay was buried outside of the temple."

The turn of the lock on the door caught my attention. His expression remained steady, and his hands settled into his pockets, like he wasn't up to mischief, though I sensed it was coming.

He neared me, his tone all business. "What explanations have you come up with?"

I stood up and offered him the seat in front of my laptop as I leaned over to configure my screen for him.

I had messily outlined three different theories to explain my findings in Notepad—nothing was ever official unless it was in Word. It was just the way of the PC universe.

He read aloud. "'Number One: Ay constructed the temple in memory of Tutankhamun.'"

"Right. That's the simplest explanation. Naturally, one would think that the patron of the temple would leave some sort of calling card, or identifier, to earn the glory of building a monument."

He propped his elbows on the armrests, his corded forearms delectably on display beneath his rolled-up sleeves. "But you don't like that explanation?"

I shook my head. "Ay resented Tutankhamun and used his short reign as a steppingstone to further his own agenda. He wouldn't pay tribute to his predecessor, a mere boy in comparison to his age, when he barely secured a tomb for him when he died." I mean, the man had even allegedly taken Tutankhamun's tomb for himself and stuffed the young king's sarcophagus and possessions into a tiny little one-room closet.

James studied me as I continued spitting out what was swirling in my brain. "And let's say that Ay really did build the temple. Why would an egomaniac like him leave a tiny statue as his signature?"

"Valid point." He hooked his arm around my waist and scooped me into his lap. The move was so suave and so James.

I planted my ass on his firm quads, my long prairie skirt flowing over his legs. His warm chest pressed into my back as we both faced my laptop.

"What's your next explanation?"

"Tutankhamun had this temple commissioned for himself."

James rested his hands on my thighs, melting them into liquid mush on contact. "But the temple was built after his death."

"Exactly—if he had commissioned it, then he would have ensured that it was finished before his death so he could approve the final appearance. And furthermore, he would have made sure it was way more extravagant than it really was."

The tip of his nose brushed my neck as his hands caressed my thighs. Butterflies fluttered in my stomach from the rhythmic touch. "And the statue?"

It was getting harder to think with him so close. "Um...maybe he was paying homage to his adviser?"

"But on the same train of thought, Ay as the adviser to a young king would have ensured that his presence was larger and more obvious than a small action figure."

"Precisely," I confirmed. My eyelids grew heavy with his movements. "Perhaps there's something more that we haven't unearthed yet," I breathed out as his hands moved higher up my leg.

"Perhaps there isn't anything else." His hand slid under my waistband and into my panties, his fingers grazing my clit. I gasped. This was what he'd had in mind, my mischievous mentor. "Next theory."

"Nefertiti," I whispered.

His hand jerked momentarily, as if I had caught him off guard with my proposal. "Explain."

I rocked my hips into his touch, urging him to continue his illicit massage.

"In addition to being Tutankhamun's stepmother, she was also believed to be the daughter of Ay." This information was redundant to James, but my brain kept short-circuiting every time he drew those perfect circles against my sensitive nub.

I leaned my head back onto his shoulder and parted my thighs wider, granting him more access. I could feel his hard cock press against my ass as I ground into his hand.

"Keep going," he encouraged. Whether he was referring to my grinding or with my explanation, I didn't know, so I continued with both.

"Maybe she wanted to honor her stepson—"

James slipped a finger inside of me, and my breath quickened. Effortlessly, he fucked my slick slit as if he were doing something as routine as checking his email.

"Ah," I moaned, my heavy eyelids falling shut. Why was I always so damn ready for this man?

"Good girl. Keep talking," he hummed into my neck.

"With a temple . . ."

His finger pumped into me as his thumb gave my clit some well-needed friction. Teeth nipped at my neck. The pent-up tension inside was driving me insane.

"And you think Nefertiti left the figurine of her father, as well as her floral bracelet, as an offering to the gods?" he said, finishing my thought.

I no longer gave a flying fuck about the temple. My needs were selfish. For all I cared right now, someone could dump sand over the entire site and erase all the progress we had made. "James, I need you," I begged.

He swiftly retreated from my panties, and I whimpered at the sudden loss. He bunched up the material of my skirt from the hem to the waist. "Stand up and hold this."

I obeyed, taking the thin fabric into my hands. Smoothly, he slipped my underwear down my legs, leaving me completely exposed.

I felt a kiss press to my bare ass. I loved how this man worshipped my body.

The sound of his zipper opening flushed a rush of excitement through me. Suddenly, my hips were guided back down slightly, and I felt his cock perfectly aligned with my desperate pussy. *Yes. This was the kind of study break I needed.*

I closed the distance the rest of the way, pushing myself down onto him. The moan that escaped my lips was far too loud and could probably have been heard from the other side of the door.

"Am I going to have to gag my kitten? Because, you know, I wouldn't mind a nice ball gag in my woman's mouth." He moved my hips up and down, impaling me with his size.

His woman? Was I really his? His meaning wasn't clear enough for me. "James, what are we doing?" I panted.

His pounding slowed slightly. "I don't know," he admitted. I could hear the uncertainty in his voice, the same that clouded my head whenever I thought about us.

"Are you mine?" I asked as I rode him.

"Only if you want me." His voice was gravelly and thick as he gave me his fat cock.

"I do." My heart was bare to him, and even if it turned out to be a mistake, I had been honest.

"Kitten," he groaned. "You're turning my world upside down, and I haven't a clue on how to navigate this."

"Then let's navigate it together." I clenched my pussy as he filled me.

"Fuck," he gritted out. "You're perfect."

I smiled to myself as I placed my hands on the table in front of me for support.

"What if we get caught?" My voice broke from the ecstasy that was building.

"I won't let that happen," he promised, his hold on my hips tightening. He was close, too.

"Angela knows," I blurted out.

He froze, and I slid down his dick, sitting on him with his erection pulsing inside of me. He deserved to know because it affected not only my position on his team but his job, as well. We were violating the code of conduct, and he had a right to be warned.

I tried to placate him. "She won't say anything."

"Did you tell her?"

"No, she figured it out." We hadn't exactly been careful enough, so it had been bound to happen. I was just glad it was Angela who knew because I was sure she'd keep my secret, especially after our talk the other day.

His fingers slid up my shirt, sliding under the cups of my bra. Rough skin scraped my sensitive nipples in the most delicious way.

"What about your boyfriend?" he asked.

"Hmmm?" I moaned.

"Felipe."

My eyes flew wide open. *Not this again.* "I already told you this. He's not my boyfriend."

"So, you told him you're not interested?" His tone was dead serious, but the way he pinched my hard nipples made it difficult to focus.

"Not exactly," I professed.

"Why not?" he snapped, squeezing my tits hard like they were water balloons.

"Ouch!" I yelped. His hands stopped moving. "He's a nice guy. I just feel bad breaking it to him."

"Do it," he warned, resuming the kind of attention my nipples desired. "Are you jealous?" I was glad I wasn't facing him, because I couldn't hide the smirk on my lips.

"Of a boy?" He moved his hands back down to my hips and lifted me quickly, then slammed me back down onto his cock, making me cry out. "No, but I don't like sharing what's mine."

I bit back my satisfied grin and let him fuck the hell out of what was his.

Chapter 21

It was funny how even when it was million degrees outside, Egyptians still drank hot tea like it was iced water. That gene must have skipped me because all I could think about drinking was a cold-ass fountain Coke from a drive-thru.

Teatime was an afternoon tradition at our site: hot black tea with a ton of sugar and flavored with fresh mint. The entire crew gathered under the tent when the sun was at its brightest and sipped their tea while chatting.

I partook in the custom but rarely finished my cup because even though it was delicious, I would just break out into a sweat the more I drank.

Angela and Sean were in the corner talking quietly as they enjoyed their drinks. They had been spending a lot of time together, and I could sense something was blooming between them. I had asked Angela if she was interested, but she'd just responded with an exaggerated, "What?!" and wide eyes. It looked like I would have to revisit the question next week.

My eyes wandered to James, who was sorting through a utility basket as he exchanged words with Mo. They must have been checking the tools to see what needed to be discarded and replaced, based on the pile of worn equipment in front of them.

His gaze caught mine, and I instantly felt my cheeks heat—and not from the tea. A faint smile spread across his lips before he turned back to his task with Mo.

"Thinking about drinking a soda instead?" Felipe took a seat next to me on the ground with his cup in hand.

I turned my head abruptly and a loose tendril of hair fell across my forehead. I smiled. "You know me too well."

"What's the first thing you're going to eat when you get back home?" he asked.

I tried to brush the hair away, but the sweat on my forehead kept it glued to its spot. "Hmmm...that's a hard one." Food in Egypt was wonderful, and the flavors were so vibrant, but I would be lying if I said I wasn't homesick for the food from home. "I'm gonna go with tamales!"

"Oh, that's a good one!"

The stray hair slid down to my eyes on a stream of sweat, and I swiped at it again with my forearm. "What are you going to eat when you get home?"

"That's easy. My mother's paella," he replied confidently. "I miss chorizo." All things "pig" were forbidden in Egypt.

I chuckled, drawing the jealous glare of our mentor.

With suddenly nervous fingers, I reached for the rogue hair that wouldn't sit still.

To my surprise, Felipe reached out and tucked it behind my ear. "There." His gentle smile twisted my stomach in an unsettling way.

"Oh...um...thanks!" I fingered the tucked away lock anxiously as if to erase his touch.

CLANK. Metal on metal. James stood over a shovel which I assumed he had slammed onto the pile of tools.

He started for us, stalking through the tent like a bull who'd just seen red.

Oh, God. Here it goes!

I locked eyes with him and widened mine, warning him to stop. He halted on the spot, crossing his arms across his chest.

I refocused my attention on Felipe, who was still smiling at me warmly and oblivious to the bull who was ready to charge him.

Now was the time. I just wished I didn't have to have this uncomfortable talk at work.

"Look, Felipe. I love spending time with you, but I want to make sure we're on the same page. You're a really great person, but I'm just not in a place where I want to be anything more than friends with a guy."

He lifted his hands in the air. "I totally get it. No need to say more. I was hoping you'd change your mind the more time we spent together, but I hear what you're saying."

I felt even more guilty for turning him down now that he'd taken it so well. In another universe, Felipe would have been the perfect guy for me. But in this one, I was more into the fuming ogre who looked just about to blow a fuse only feet away. "You're not mad?"

"A little disappointed, sure. But not mad. I appreciate your honesty."

"Thanks for understanding." I smiled.

I watched as James's anger cooled from a rolling boil to a bubbling simmer before he headed back to play with his little toys with Mo. For a grown man, he could be such a child.

***

Two hours and half of a bottle of water later, I set to work inside of the temple to inspect the hieroglyphs again in search of any clues as to who was responsible for the monument.

Shoes crunched on the ground behind me. I knew who it was from the intentional steps.

My concentration remained fixed on the wall in front of me, my flashlight propped on the utility table shedding steady light on my subject of study.

Debris snapped under his shifting weight and I felt his heated stare on my neck, but I didn't address his presence.

"Did you talk to him?" The arrogance in his tone sent my eyes rolling so hard in my head that they were seriously in danger of sticking, if Mom's lifelong theory were to be believed.

I wasn't turning around until he fixed his attitude. I had done nothing wrong, and I wasn't going to encourage his behavior.

"Hello to you, too, *Dr. Campbell.*"

"Did you talk to him?" he growled again.

I pretended to write something so very important in my notebook that I couldn't possibly tear my attention from it. "Talk to whom?"

"*Sanura,*" he hissed.

"*James,*" I hissed back.

His fingers dug into my elbow as he spun me around. Wild eyes burned in the dim lighting. "Don't do that."

I pulled my arm from his grasp. "Do what?"

"Act like a child."

The laugh that cracked from my chest sounded slightly manic. "You're the one slamming tools because you can't control your jealousy, and I'm the child?" I kept my voice low, though I wanted to scream at the top of my lungs. The last thing I needed was for the rest of the team to run in here from all the commotion.

"He was touching you."

"Correction: he was touching my *hair*." I admit the move had been mildly flirtatious, but I wasn't about to say that to Mr. Irrational.

"According to the internship ethics committee, no man is allowed to touch a woman unless he's married to her."

He had to be kidding. "Asshole, you weren't too worried about ethics when your dick was balls-deep in my pussy in a study room only twenty feet away from the dean's office."

James took a large step toward me, but I pulled away. "Don't come closer."

"So now you don't want me near you?" he said huskily. He took another unwanted step.

I stepped backward again, desperate to keep space between us. "Not when you're acting like this."

"Kitten, if you don't like my behavior, you only have yourself to blame, because you drive me fucking mad."

I took another step back, and my ass bumped into the fold-out utility table behind me. "You're fucking insane."

"That's right, beautiful. Insane for you." He'd cornered me. He dipped his head, and I felt his warm breath on my neck.

I took a fortifying breath, unwilling to let lust sway me so easily. "You need to trust me."

His fingers teased the neckline of my sweaty T-shirt. "I trust you, but I don't trust *him*."

"Didn't you select him as your intern?" He knew more about Felipe than Felipe probably even knew about himself from the extensive background check that we had all been required to submit to before selection.

Instead of replying, he dropped his gaze. His tongue swiped over his bottom lip as his hungry eyes raked over my chest.

"I told him, not that I owe you an explanation."

James pried my notebook and pen out of my hands and tossed them aside. His nuzzled my sweaty neck, licking my skin. "You must have broken his little pretty-boy heart."

My eyes darted to the temple door, making sure the entrance was clear. I couldn't hear any voices or footsteps nearby. Tilting my head back, I gave in to him. "You're so dramatic."

He bit the skin on my neck hard.

"Ouch!" I hissed, rubbing my wound. "Are you crazy? We're in the middle of work and I have no way to hide this if it bruises!" The last thing we needed was to walk out of this temple together with hickeys on my neck.

He pulled my hand away and spun me around, so my chest was flat on the table.

Panic overtook me with the door no longer in my range of sight. "James, what are you doing?"

"Teaching you that you're mine to do whatever the hell I want with."

Quickly, he worked the zipper on my jeans and pushed everything down, including my panties.

He captured both of my wrists behind my back and held them in place as he hunched over me and whispered, "Keep your hands still; otherwise, I'll give you more marks that you'll have to account for."

A quick slap of my ass sent a stinging sensation pulsing through my flesh that I felt deep in my core.

Suddenly, he slammed into my pussy, filling me with his cock. He pounded into me, not giving me a moment to adjust to his size.

Our sweaty skin slapped together. The sand kicked up from our movements created a suffocating storm around us. It was dirty. It was crazy. It was perfectly us.

Bent over and fucking like animals in this place of worship felt so wrong, but I couldn't stop. Our depravity was out there for the pharaoh and all his gods to see. The taboo nature of it all just made my pussy drip wetter all over his dick.

"I need you to get there, kitten," James gritted out, releasing my hands. We had been alone for far too long; I knew it was only a matter of seconds before someone walked in on us.

I frantically rubbed my fingers against my clit, bringing myself to the edge release.

"Are you close?" he panted.

"Yes. I'm almost—"

His pace quickened, movements uneven. My hips knocked against the edge of the table.

Voices neared us. Then the sound of rocks under shoes.

"Fuck," he ground out.

With one final slam into me, he filled my slit with hot cum, which sent me spiraling under him. My mouth opened in a silent scream.

Just as suddenly as it had begun, James pulled out of me and dressed himself. I quickly followed suit, with no time to register the soreness of my hips from banging against the table.

A moment later, Mo walked into the temple.

"We need your help with the perimeter," he said to James without giving me a second glance.

Wordlessly, James walked out with him, leaving me to catch my breath in private.

Chapter 22

I never thought the day would come where I would be celebrating Isabella Bianchi's twenty-first birthday. And if you had told me that I'd be slamming down shots and dancing with her, then I'd have accused you of leaning in too close when using a permanent marker.

But here I was, shaking my ass to Bad Bunny with my arm around Isabella like we were BFFs en route to scoring matching tattoos. Life was a crazy bitch.

The club, technically a lounge, was a surprising change of pace from the Egypt I had experienced so far. I spent my days immersed in the land of the dead, digging through sand in hopes of finding remnants of the past—or even a dead person, if I was lucky. But tonight, it felt good to party in the land of the living.

A live DJ played the hottest songs, a mix of worldwide hits, as the crowd danced and drank the night away. Our entire group looked damn good in the middle of the dance floor, too. We had all gone shopping for new outfits just for the occasion. Sean and Felipe looked hot in their button-downs and jeans with drinks in hand. Angela looked gorgeous as usual, and her fresh blowout made her hair extra bouncy as she dropped it low to the ground. Even Isabella looked fucking fantastic in her sparkly silver jumpsuit, like a sexy disco ball. Who'd have known that she had a killer body under all that obnoxiousness?! And the girl could dance like she was on spring break in Cancun.

I felt cute in my dress, too. I had been thrilled when I'd stumbled across this emerald-green wrap dress with long cuffed sleeves. The hem skimmed my knees, yet it still hugged my body in all the right ways. The neckline wasn't overly provocative but still gave me the illusion of cleavage without being too much. The only miss was that I had worn my ballet flats with it instead of splurging on heels. My ankle was back to normal but I hadn't wanted to risk having another mishap just to gain four inches in height, especially when alcohol would be involved.

Angela had been kind enough to do my makeup, which she'd totally slayed. The smokey eye played up the almond shape of my eyes, while the mild contouring highlighted my high cheekbones. I'd opted for a nude-pink lip to keep the look on the subtler side. My hair was rather simple, too, with just a gold hair clip on one side of my head, allowing my curls to cascade over one shoulder.

I looked fierce. We all did, and we knew it, judging by how hard we worked the dance floor.

Angela and Sean were awfully cozy, with his leg sandwiched between Angela's thighs as she ground into him. Her arms were wrapped around his neck and their faces were barely visible, but I was pretty sure they were making out by now. If anyone else had noticed, they didn't let on; everyone was too distracted to care.

Ordinarily, public displays of horniness didn't abide by the country's social etiquette, but in the lounge, nobody seemed to care. It was a safe space to let loose and let down our guards.

Isabella donned the tiara of Birthday Girl well—she had climbed up onto the bar and was dancing for a group that cheered her on from below. This wouldn't last long, because when the clock struck twelve, she'd turn back into a grouchy pumpkin and probably deny any of this had ever happened.

I might have gotten carried away with my liquor consumption, too, because I couldn't remember what number shot I was currently about to shoot. Three, four...seven. It was all a damn blur, and I was losing my balance. I grabbed onto Felipe's arm to save myself from face-planting.

He wrapped his arm around my waist, his body forming a wall to steady me. It was purely platonic, and I didn't feel the least bit uncomfortable by his touch. Even though Felipe and I weren't a couple, we had become great friends. And I knew he understood my position on wanting to remain friends, because I had watched him dance with a few girls and even exchanged numbers with them earlier.

"You okay?" he shouted into my ear from behind, just as Doja Cat's "Woman" blared around us.

I swayed to the music, maybe a little more from the effects of the vodka, but I just couldn't keep still.

I turned my head to look over my shoulder, my hands resting on the masculine forearm around my waist. "Yeah! Just a little dehydrated!"

"Want some water?" he asked.

I shook my head. "I want to keep dancing." I was addicted to the vibe. I didn't ever want this night to end.

We continued to move in unison, singing along to Doja Cat offering to be some guy's woman.

My eyes roamed from the sweaty crowd to Isabella still on the bar, this time with a bottle in hand as she lip-synched along, too. I took in the upper level, where the VIP guests were having their own party, dancing and chatting over drinks.

Through my drunken haze, my eyes caught on something familiar staring down at me. Thick mussed hair over stone-like eyes glaring at me. The same face that I pictured every night under the covers, wishing Angela weren't asleep in the same room so I could use my fingers to ease the ache his body spurred between my legs.

I shook my head and looked again. He was gone.

There was no way James could be here. Ever the workaholic, he was most likely holed up in his office, pouring over his notes.

"Bathroom!" I shouted to Felipe. He nodded before releasing me. I needed to splash some cold water on my neck because I had clearly drunk too much if I was hallucinating that my non-boyfriend teacher fuckbuddy was glaring down at me like Anubis, the guardian of the underworld, ready to weigh my heart and judge me.

I trod through the throngs of people, with the occasional shoulder or ass bumping into me.

The hallway to the women's restroom had a long line, and my bladder couldn't wait. My eyes bounced upstairs to the unmanned red ropes. *VIP.* They had to have a bathroom I could use. No one would even know if I slipped through, especially since the bouncer was MIA.

I slowly backed out of the line and made a beeline up the stairs to the ropes. I slid to the side of them and traveled down the dark hall until I found the door I was looking for.

I pressed the gold handle, and the door opened to a private bathroom with fancy red-and-black wallpaper and mood lighting. This was the VIP life...never having to share a bathroom. *Must be nice to pee in luxury!*

I locked the door and quickly emptied my bladder before it burst and then washed my hands. The squeaky-clean mirror in front me made no qualms about displaying my sweaty skin and smudged eyes. I pressed the cool water to my neck and chest to cure my hyperthermia. Relief washed over me, and some of my senses returned.

I needed to get a hold of myself because this obsession with James was unhealthy. It was one thing to think about him all the time, but now I was seeing him when he wasn't there.

The handle suddenly clicked, and before I could register what was happening, the door flew open.

"James!"

He stood there with legs planted wide, fists clenched at his sides. Tendons bulged below his rolled-up sleeves. Already a tall man, he looked to have gained another foot just from how stiff his posture was.

"What are you doing in here?" I didn't know whether to be horrified that he'd just picked a bathroom lock when I could have still been on the toilet or to be relieved that I hadn't been losing my mind and hallucinating earlier.

His nostrils flared and the breath that escaped them came out in a deep grunt. "Why was he touching you?" His voice sounded tight, like he was seconds away from exploding.

Here we go again. I couldn't keep having this same argument about Felipe, especially not when I was inebriated.

I lifted my hands, signaling I was done, and stepped around him to leave. In one swoop, he grabbed my arm and pulled me back, pressing my ass against the edge of the counter. I was stuck with his rough hand holding my chin in place and his hips pinning me in.

With all my might, I shoved against his chest, but he didn't move. "Let me go, James! I can't do this again. My head is swimming and I need water."

He angled his nose down to my mouth and inhaled my breath. Those beautiful cobalt eyes that I loved were dark like stone. "You're fucking drunk."

I cackled. "For someone so smart, it sure does take you long to figure out the obvious, huh?"

Suddenly, he flipped me so my lower belly was rammed against the edge of the counter. My palms flew to the surface for balance. I was hunched over, staring at our reflection: me, breathless, and him, a monster ready to rage.

"Leave me alone!" I wriggled to break free of his arm wrapped around my chest, but I was just too out of it to fight properly. "Why are you here? Shouldn't you be digging shit up?"

He buried his nose in my hair. His cock was hard and pressing into me, reminding me of the dirty things it was capable of. "Birthday party for Blossom," he grunted.

"Who?" I bit out, trying to keep from rubbing against him. His erection was clouding my judgment more than the alcohol.

"Dr. Moore," he hummed, tickling my skin with the tip of his nose.

My body went rigid like he had electrocuted me with just that one name.

That fucking bitch?

And instantly, I was ready for Round Two.

"You should go back to your *colleague*." Emphasis on "colleague," with none of the meaning. I bucked him with my ass, but instead of pushing him away, it just ended up grinding against his dick.

"Stop worrying about her. She's married...happily."

So, there it was, Dr. Moore was a married woman. Relief flooded my body. But I was still angry about his hate for Felipe.

His body bent over mine, and his hand lifted the hem of my dress high enough to rub himself against my full cheeks exposed by my thong.

Unwanted desire flickered to life in my core as I watched his jaw clench as he worked me.

"I want that boy to stop touching what's mine," he groaned.

I had difficulty remembering why I was so upset with him when all I could think about was how I wanted him to direct his attention to my aching pussy.

I leaned further forward, angling my hips back so he could hit my covered yet swollen lips with his motion. The sensation was nearly enough to make me combust. "He's just a friend."

He ripped my panties down my legs, then smoothed my cheeks with his hand before administering a hard slap. "Do you let your friends grind their cocks into your ass, too?"

"No, only asshole professors who go around swinging their dicks to prove they're better than college boys." He might have had my pussy, but I would take his ego.

Suddenly, his zipper released and without hesitation, he slammed into me, lurching my body forward.

We cried out in unison at the impact. No more fighting. No more resisting. There was just this—our primal need for one another.

His ministrations weren't gentle, and I didn't want them to be. I wanted him to use me, to take his anger out on me.

His skin slapped against mine as he railed me from behind. Sex had never been this good, nor would it ever be this good again. I would mourn this relationship when it was over and would always wonder what could have been.

Would I hate him for the way things ended when they inevitably did? Would he miss me? Would we ever run into each other again?

There were so many unknowns that scared me, but it scared me more to ask the questions that troubled me.

Tonight, we were simply together, and I would relish that fact.

He yanked the neckline of my dress down, exposing my bra, and roughly pulled the cups down, releasing my tits from their bondage. He palmed one of the shaking mounds.

Our breaths were erratic as we watched ourselves fucking like animals in the mirror before us. Every twitch of muscle...every bead of sweat...every expression yearning for more. We saw it all.

"Oh, James. Fuck me harder, baby."

His eyes were bright again, just how I loved them—wild with desire just for me. "You like it when I stuff your tight little hole?"

I nodded, begging for more. "Yes. Please."

The hand that had been pinching my nipple slid down to my clit. The sight of his hand between my legs, working tight circles on my nub, sent a thrill down my spine.

His other hand gripped my hip as he continued to pound into me mercilessly. The man could fuck like a god.

My moans were growing louder and coming closer together. I was so fucking close.

James worked me harder, anxious to see me through to the end like a king. And I was his fucking queen.

I was there, ready to fall over the edge and take him with me.

"Baby, I'm going to—"

But then he pulled out and quickly did his zipper, leaving me empty and cold.

I spun around to face him, my tits still hanging out and juices sliding down my legs. "What the fuck are you doing?" The cry was rabid.

He tucked his shirt into his pants and just like that looked like he hadn't just been balls-deep inside of me. "Come home with me tonight."

"What? I can't leave my friends." I hit his chest with my fist. "And why the fuck did you stop?"

He cuffed my chin with his hand, eyes dark like midnight. "If you want me to make your pretty little cunt squirt, then come home with me." It was an order—one that would force me away from Felipe for the rest of the night, just like he wanted.

He was an asshole who expected to get his way in everything. But I was tipsy and my pussy hurt too much to resist. And there was no way in hell I was sending him with this hard-on back into that club full of hot women ready to throw themselves at him.

Righting my bra and dress with one hand, I pulled my phone out of my pocket with the other, and he released my chin.

I texted Angela. *I'm going home with James. Cover for me from the crew, please.*

Holy shit. He's here? came her reply almost instantly.

Yep.

And he wants some of that ass, tonight?

I rolled my eyes and texted again, *Yep.*

Well, then, don't make the man wait. Go bone him.

I slipped my phone back into my pocket. "Let's go," I ground out, hating that I had let my pussy win over my brain.

Chapter 23

As soon as we walked through the door to James's place, clothes were ripped off, tongues were tangled, and hands were touching every part that yearned for attention.

Our naked bodies were inseparable, like we were permanently fused together as one. My lips parted wide, giving his tongue uninhibited access to my mouth. Our kisses were messy and frenetic, the kind of needy ones you saw in pornos, but ours weren't for show. We couldn't get our fill of one another.

James lifted me, and I wrapped my legs around his hard waist. With jarring force, he rammed me against the wall, and I was sure I'd end up with a bruise tomorrow. His strong arms held me in place under my ass as we continued to consume each other. It was like a competition to see how far we could reach our tongues down each other's throats.

My slick pussy slid along the smoothness of his dick where it protruded between my legs as he knocked me about in our reckless haze of lust.

"If you don't fuck me now, I'll report you to the ministry for harassment," I demanded between kisses.

He smiled against my mouth. "You wouldn't dare."

"Try me." I bit into his lip, eliciting a panty-dropping groan—if I'd still had them on. *The professor likes it rough.*

He smothered my neck with open-mouthed kisses, tasting my skin. "God, kitten. You're fucking perfect for me." And he was for me. Perfectly mercurial, stubborn, and a hell of a lover.

I writhed against him, my need robbing me of the ability to think properly. "Please, James! Fuck my cunt." My demand was harsh, but I was desperate for release.

He sucked in a breath at my choice of words. "How can I resist when you ask so nicely?" Suddenly, I was whisked upstairs to his room and tossed onto his bed. I landed with a bounce against the mattress.

His body was so cut from digging in the sand all day that I could see every muscle flex in his arms as he crawled up my body. He rained kisses on my lips and neck before moving lower. Calloused hands gripped my tits firmly as his tongue traced circles over my aching nipples, flicking the peaks.

My pussy couldn't handle any more of this torture. She needed to be loved...to be hurt.

But he continued with his kisses down my belly.

I huffed a large breath and shoved him as hard as I could. Taken by surprise, he landed on his back next to me.

In the blink of an eye, I was on him, one hand around the base of his shaft and the other on his chest for balance. I fed his cock into my hungry hole, impaling myself with his massive length. With my knees on either side of him, I began to move, taking exactly what I needed, when I needed it.

"Oh, fuck," he gasped. His length slipped inside me easily from how wet we both were for each other. "You're so greedy for me."

I rode him hard, my tits bouncing as I found my rhythm. His hands traveled from my waist to my breasts, massaging them in his massive palms.

The feeling of him against my walls drove me mad. He was lost in the moment, too, judging by his guttural moans. His neck muscles were tight with ecstasy. I bent down and ran my tongue along his jugular vein, feeling it pulse under my taste.

"You're hurting me so good, baby," I moaned. "I feel you so deep inside."

The pad of his thumb rubbed against my lower lip. "This fucking mouth," he groaned. "It'll be the death of me."

It was true—in and out of the bedroom. It made me wonder if he would find another woman who challenged him as much as I did when our relationship was over. Blocking out the sadness that I felt, I tilted my pelvis back slightly and moved faster—forgetting my worries.

He let out a strained sound, signaling he was close. "Kitten, I won't last much longer."

I milked him until I felt his shaft swell and my hole tighten. He was ready to explode, and that was when I struck. I ripped myself off him and jumped off the bed, leaving his wet erection standing proud but very lonely.

"What the fuck?!" he growled. It was an angry and feral cry. The kind a beast made when it was no longer in control.

All I did was grin, standing there with my hands on my hips. "It doesn't feel so nice, does it?" *He wasn't the only one who knew how to use sex as a weapon.*

"Is this payback for earlier?" he shouted. *My angry professor.* "Sanura, get back here and finish what you started." He reached for me, but I slinked away.

"Do unto others as you would have them do unto you," I sang. "Maybe you should have played nice at the club—I would have been *so* nice to you right now." Withholding orgasm from me was the cruelest thing he could have done, and he needed to know what it felt like. *Good luck with the blue balls, buddy.*

"Stop quoting the Bible and bring that pussy here." His face was turning darker shades of red by the second.

"No." I crossed my arms over my breasts. "Stop throwing Felipe in my face. We're just friends!"

"Sanura!" he warned, kneeling on the bed. His hand cupped his aching balls.

"Uh-uh. Not with that tone." He wasn't about to boss me around when he was being the dick. I ran my finger lazily down my belly, grazing my soft hair at the end of the journey.

His beautiful lapis lazuli eyes followed my hand, ready to attack at any moment. His tone softened. "Please, kitten. I'll never bring him up again."

God, I loved hearing him beg for a change. It sent twinges to my swollen lips. But I continued my torture, dipping a finger inside of my aching slit, complemented by an emphatic moan from my lips.

He watched me through heavy lids, stroking his length as I fucked myself with my finger. "What do you want from me? I'll do anything for you."

I squeezed my heavy tit with my other hand, continuing my self-love. Our juices inside of me made sticky noises with every pump of my finger. "You want me like this?" I hummed.

His eyes held onto mine. "Always." And somehow, I thought he might have meant more than just physically. At least, I hoped.

I pulled my finger out and held it up for him to see our glistening arousal before sucking it off. The marriage of our flavors brought my taste buds to life.

James growled and palmed his balls as if the sight had physically pained him.

It was time to put the man out of his misery. "Lie down."

He obliged with his head on the pillow. I didn't straddle his hips like before. Instead, I perched myself over his face, with my knees opened wide around his head so he could reach me.

"Lick me," I ordered.

His whole face brightened at my command, and he obeyed without protest. "Happy to be of service."

One swipe of his tongue on my clit and I was doubled over with pleasure. I held onto the headboard as he massaged me with the tip of his tongue. Steady, even strokes like he was strumming a guitar and hitting all the right notes.

I crouched lower to hold onto his head. I wound my hips to match his tempo, grinding into his face, my tightly coiling pleasure just waiting to release.

I weaved my fingers into his thick hair, yanking on it hard. It probably hurt, but he had proven himself worthy of the pain.

His tongue swiped at my slit, hindering my balance on already shaky knees. Rough hands skated up my belly and kneaded my breasts.

I was lost in the strokes of his tongue, all my senses fading except my strengthening sense of touch. My inner thighs chaffed deliciously from his stubble. "Don't stop, baby," I breathed out.

He didn't. He gave me more, dipping two fingers inside and fucking me way better than I had fucked myself. I could feel my walls contract around the welcome intrusion. How was it possible that he knew my body better than me?

Suddenly, the warmth disappeared from my pussy. His tongue continued to work my clit as his sticky fingers slid between my ass cheeks. I froze.

No one had ever been back there, and to be honest, I wasn't ready for it tonight.

But his fingers never entered me. Instead, they massaged my tight entrance. My body relaxed into a blissful moan. The feeling was unreal—like hundreds of nerve endings coming alive all at once.

Fireworks exploded, and I detonated into pieces, screaming his name. I'd never felt like this with anyone. The rush he gave me was addicting. I was already having withdrawals, thinking about leaving his bed in the morning.

My knees gave out and I collapsed back onto his chest. He looked so fucking sexy with my arousal smeared over his satisfied grin.

He wiped my wetness off his chin with his upper arm and pegged me with his eyes.

"My turn." Like lightning, he flipped me onto my back, my head at the bottom of the bed. The caveman threw one of my legs over his shoulder and plunged inside of me without invitation. I had yet to recover from my own high, and his massive size only heightened my sensitivity.

James pounded, rolling his hips as he made contact with my nub. He didn't just fuck me, he worked my pussy raw. My eyes disappeared into my head as he bumped me closer and closer to the edge of the bed, until my head was hanging over.

I wanted this forever, to be his and for him to be mine. I needed it more than I needed air. Our joined bodies felt more right than anything I had haver experienced in my life. He had to feel it, too. The way that he was looking at me now through heavy lids, like he was worshipping all of me...he had to have felt it.

Rigid stone scraped my fingertips as I ran them down his abs. His golden skin was damp with perspiration.

His jaw clenched and his body tensed. Our movements became wild and untamable. It was only us in this moment. No internship. No ethics.

He shouted his climax while arching his back, filling me with his warm seed before crashing onto me. We were a sticky, sweaty, sweet mess.

This man, the one whose heart was beating furiously against mine, was everything I hadn't known I needed. I had fallen for him, and there was no returning from it. My obsession with him was more than just physical. It was whole and consuming. It was *love*.

Chapter 24

When I was younger, I had loved puzzles. I'd spent hours assembling them. The more pieces the box had, the more motivated I had been to complete it. My favorite had been a giant circus scene with various breeds of dogs doing random tricks like jumping through hoops and balancing on giant balls. It had taken me nearly a week to assemble all five thousand pieces. After I'd finished, I hadn't had the heart to break it apart and store it in the box, so instead, Mom had framed and hung it over my dresser as a reminder of what I could accomplish.

Puzzles weren't a team sport. Sure, the more people who participated, the faster it would be completed. But part of the intrigue for me had always been that I could work on it by myself, marinate over the pieces at my own pace, and try to fit them together even if the combinations were obviously wrong without ever having to explain my reasoning. *Trial and error.*

It was the perfect activity for an only child.

Archaeology was like solving a giant puzzle. There were lots of little pieces or clues to discover, and my job was to fit them all together to reveal the bigger picture.

Time had ticked away too quickly for the dig. There was only a week and a half left on James's permit, and we'd made no headway on figuring out the patron of the temple. I was still adamant that it was a woman, but no new evidence had turned up to support my claim. It was the hardest puzzle I had ever worked to solve, and there were no Pomeranians balancing on tightropes in this one.

My eyes were officially beginning to cross from how long I had been reviewing my notes inside of the temple.

The bracelet I had found was still at the lab being analyzed, and the ministry hadn't renewed the project for next year's season yet, either. It wasn't a hard no, but if we finished empty-handed in the next ten days, it was very probable that James's work on this temple would be over, even though he had discovered it.

The stress was getting to him. Though he never admitted it, I could just tell. His shoulders were always tensed under his ears. He wasn't a smiler in general, but his frowns had deepened, and the little wrinkles that he had gained from sun exposure were more prominent. I could feel the worry in his kiss and in his touch. I wished I could take it all away and find the answers he needed.

Even if I could, my own dark cloud would still loom over me. Whether or not we found any answers about the dig, I was still going home soon, and I didn't know where I stood with James. That was perhaps the most difficult part of this puzzle—the pieces that made up my heart. I didn't want to ask questions and turn over pieces only to find out that they didn't fit together. My soul couldn't take it.

I hadn't expected to fall as hard as I had for James. This was meant to have just been a fling. A panty-soaking trope that I could check off my bucket list.

James never broached the topic, either. Did he even feel the same way about me? When we were together, I was convinced he did, but his continued silence on the topic led me to believe otherwise. Maybe he didn't want to discuss it because he wanted a clean break from me when the internship was over.

My chest ached thinking about packing up my stuff and leaving him behind, but I supposed all good things must eventually come to an end.

And to make matters more depressing, I had no news about the search for my uncle from the private investigator. I had spoken to Aaqil three days ago, and he'd said that he was still searching. I had abandoned hope that I'd get to meet my family before I left.

Why did I always have to lose the things that I loved? *Reminder: Call Mom and make sure she's still alive and breathing. If I lose her too, they'll surely need to mummify me on the spot.*

The weight on my shoulders was too heavy to bear, and my hands itched for something physical as a distraction. I slammed my notebook shut and scraped at the sand with my trowel furiously.

"You're going to kill your wrist if you keep going like that." James peered at me from the doorway with his arms crossed over his chest. The material of his white shirt clung to his biceps.

I threw my tool aside and rubbed my wrist. He was right...it was already sore. "What does it matter? I'll be home for the rest of the semester and summer doing nothing soon anyway."

The sour note in my tone earned me a raised eyebrow, but he stayed rooted to the spot.

My head felt heavy, like there was a knot just above my brow. I rubbed at it to release some of the tension. "Do you need me for something?" I huffed out, unable to hide my irritation.

He took a seat on the ground next to me. "Did I do something?" he asked, his voice deepening.

I tried to brush him off. All the thoughts that raced in my head were getting to me. "I just needed some space to work."

His fingers lifted my chin. "Kitten, talk to me." The light from my flashlight bounced against the deep blue of his eyes.

I didn't want to have this conversation at work, but too much of my stress was bubbling over and I was about to combust from worry. "What are we doing?"

He didn't answer, but from the way that his brows fell and his shoulders sagged, he knew what I was referring to.

It was already out there floating between us now, so I continued. "I leave in ten days."

He diverted his eyes to the pit in front of us, his fingers toying with the sand. "I know."

"James. What do you want to happen?"

He let out a sigh. "In an ideal world, I would never have met you."

The words struck me as if he had slapped my face. *He regretted us.*

"If I hadn't met you, then I wouldn't be straining to find ways to make you stay."

My eyes darted to his for any hint of humor or sarcasm. But they were intense and honest.

"Y-you want me to stay?" I stuttered.

"Did you want to leave and end things?" Insecurity perforated his voice.

All I could do was laugh—snort, really. I had been so worried that I was just another notch in his headboard, and this man was worried that I wanted to leave him without a goodbye.

"I don't see what's so funny." Now, he was the one who was annoyed.

I grabbed his wrist attempting to steady my fit. "I'm not laughing at you. I'm just surprised that you want me to stay."

He cocked his head to one side, still not comprehending.

"James. You're the smartest man in the field. You should be with someone who is at your caliber. Like Dr. Moore."

"Sanura," he groaned in warning.

"I know, I know. She's happily married." I hadn't brought her up because I was jealous this time. "I just meant that you need someone more educated and traveled than an undergraduate student. I still eat cold pizza from the fridge on my way to class, for God's sake. You should be dining on caviar with super-smart professors."

"I hate caviar," he said plainly. "I'd rather the cold pizza."

I chuckled.

His fingers intertwined with mine. "I don't think I can let you go."

I didn't want to go. I wanted to remain by his side.

His free hand continued to play at the sand, raking it as he gripped my hand with the other.

I leaned my head onto his shoulder. "Then don't let me go," I whispered.

He pulled away from me, surprised by my response. The connection in our stare was like steel. *Unbreakable.* I didn't know how this would work, but I wanted to figure it out—with him.

Now was the time to let him know how I truly felt. That I had fallen madly in love with him and that I was his. My heart would burst if I didn't tell him.

"James, I lo—"

Suddenly, a pebble clanked against something in the dirt hole, stealing our attention. We both leaned in to see what it was.

Gold.

A small gold block with uneven edges, worn and broken over time.

"What is it?" I asked.

James grabbed a brush and removed some of the sediment on it to reveal more of its surface, then gingerly picked it up and placed it in his palm under the light.

Faint engraving in the metal could be seen at first glance. James brushed it some more to make it more visible.

Flowers bordered the edge of the block, intricately engraved. A series of hieroglyphs adorned the center.

I read them— "Ankhesenamun?" King Tutankhamun's wife and half-sister. I looked at James. "What is her cartouche doing here?"

Brows drawn, James shook his head as if trying to place why.

My brain worked, compiling data from the past two months. The childhood scenes on the temple wall of King Tutankhamun playing in a garden with his sisters. The figurine of Ay. The bracelet with the same flower design on the hook.

These flowers, they seemed familiar. I had seen them in a textbook. A scene with Ankhesenamun gifting her husband flowers.

I flipped the block over in his hands to reveal more hieroglyphs. I read them slowly in my head: *Loyal wife, guardian of the memory of the Great King of Wisdom.* "King of Wisdom" was Tutankhamun's title.

I grabbed his forearm. "James."

His attention was no longer on the block.

"The temple. Ankhesenamun. She's the patron."

It all made sense. She had built this temple for her husband. The figurine of Ay was here because he'd later forced her to marry him after

Tutankhamun's death. She must have built this temple in secret while she was married to Ay and had tried to use him as a decoy to keep anyone from finding out she was responsible for the temple.

James stared at me like I had just won the lottery—a mixture of shock and amazement.

I squealed as I jostled his shoulders, the excitement too much to handle. "She built the temple!"

"I can't believe it," he said, shaking his head. "All this time, it was her."

I climbed onto his lap, straddling his hips, and cupped his face in my hands. "We did it!"

Grinning, he placed the block gently beside us and held onto my waist. "*You* did it."

Our lips fused in a celebratory kiss, the rush of our discovery electrifying the air around us. I opened my mouth, inviting him in to take all of me. All the hard work and struggle had been worth it.

Our tongues tangled enthusiastically as we released the strain and un-certainty of the past few weeks. My fingers weaved into his hair, tugging on it slightly as the intensity of our celebration increased. His hands snaked up my waist, riding underneath the hem of my shirt. The roughness of the sand still on his palms abraded my skin. My pussy wanted him. It always wanted him. Just as his hard bulge wanted me. I undulated my hips on his lap, help-ing myself to some much-needed friction. His fingertips gripped into my skin as he moved me against his cock. I let the man I loved consume my mouth. I was his, and even though I hadn't gotten to say it properly for the first time, I was certain he knew it.

"Kitten, my brilliant girl," he hummed against my lips.

I couldn't hide my smile. Everything was so right. For the first time in my life, I felt like I belonged. I was meant to be here with James.

"James...I never want this to end," I whispered.

He tugged on my lower lip with his teeth. "I won't let it."

"Oh, my God!"

Our heads snapped to the entrance of the temple, which we had stupidly left open. James and I ripped away from each other as fast as if lightning had struck between us.

Isabella. She stood gawking at us in disbelief. Her hands covered her mouth as she stumbled backward.

I swiped at my lips with the back of my hand, as if that would erase what she had just seen. Scrunching my eyes shut, I prayed that this was all just a terrible nightmare. When I blinked my eyes open, Isabella was still there, her glare darting between James and me in horror.

My heart hammered so hard in my chest that it felt like my ribs would break from the pressure.

Fuck. How could we have been so irresponsible?

I sat on the ground, shaking, waiting for her to do something—scream, curse me out, throw a rock, anything. But she just stood there, eyes gaping and completely mute, almost a mirror of my own expression.

James made the first move. He stood up, maintaining a straight spine and lifted chin. His body language was steady and controlled, like he was trying not to startle her. He took two careful steps toward her, but she backed away like a frightened cat.

"Isabella." His tone was gentle.

"I have to go!" she squeaked and ran out of the temple, nearly tripping to get away from us.

"Shit. Shit. Shit," I repeated over and over, holding my head while rocking back and forth. "This is bad. This is bad."

"It's going to be okay." James was staring at the entrance. He looked like a robot just spitting out consolations.

"What are you talking about?!" I tried my best to keep my voice at a whisper, but the words crackled as they came out. "Isabella is going to blab to everyone!"

Of all the people to walk in on us, it had to be Ms. Goody Two-Shoes. She was probably on her way to file a formal complaint to the ministry.

But then again, we had bonded at her birthday party, so maybe she felt a sort of kinship with me. I had let her suck a lime out of my mouth, for God's sake! I prayed that for once in her life, she'd obey girl code and keep her mouth shut.

"Sanura. Breathe."

"How can you be so damn calm? Our careers are on the line! You could be fired, and I could never have a career to begin with if she says anything."

"I'm not afraid of her, and you shouldn't be, either." His reassurances were getting on my damn nerves.

"Afraid?" My voice came out high-pitched and maniacal. "I'm not afraid. Who says I'm afraid? It's no big deal that the most competitive person on the team saw your hand up my shirt. No big deal at all." I brushed my hand through the air, doing a terrible impression of 'nonchalant Kitty.' Kitty was not nonchalant right now. Not one bit.

He put his hand on my chest. "You need to take a deep breath."

"Okay. Okay. Breathe. Right." I sucked in a sharp breath and forced it out even faster, which didn't help at all. Instead, I wanted to pass out.

James took my wrists in his hand. "Calm down. Panicking isn't going to make any of this better." His touch was careful and not intimate in the least, like he was trying to put distance between us. I could already feel him slipping away.

Tears stung my eyes. "What do we do now?" I said, my voice trembling.

The expression in his eyes was direct. "We face the music."

My eyes nearly popped out of my skull. "What?! No. We can't go out there. Please don't make me go out there." I couldn't show my face after this. The humiliation of being known as the slutty intern who'd fucked her mentor behind her team's back would eat me alive. I wouldn't be allowed to graduate if the ethics committee found out, nor would another university ever accept me to finish up my degree.

James gently swung my arms in an attempt to break me from my oncoming panic attack. "Sanura. We can't stay in here forever."

Sanura. He kept calling me by name, and all I wanted was to hear him say "kitten" with the adoration he'd had only minutes ago, before we'd been discovered. I was already losing everything that I had only just begun to cherish.

He gave my hands a soft squeeze and offered me a tight smile that didn't quite reach his blue eyes.

He let go of me, and my heart lurched forward, grieving the loss.

I watched through blurry eyes as he bent over and slipped the golden cartouche that bore the name of a queen who had run out of options into a small specimen bag and placed it in his pocket.

He straightened up and stepped closer to the door. One more step over the threshold, and he was no longer mine. It wasn't supposed to end like this. It wasn't supposed to end.

"James," I called out.

He turned back, his brows narrowed as if he were saying his final goodbye. Then he stepped out of the temple.

I swiped at my tears and hurried out behind him. My eyes adjusted to the blaring sun to find the entire team lined up, glaring at James.

Footsteps scurried to my side. *Angela.* "Oh, babe. Are you okay?" she whispered, throwing her arm around me.

Words wouldn't form. I just shook my head.

"She told everyone," she said, referring to Isabella.

I cast my eyes to the ground in shame. Shame that everyone knew the private details of my personal life.

Mo approached James, his face void of its usual jovial expression. He stared his boss in the eye. "Leave now."

James didn't flinch. "No."

Mo stepped closer, invading James's space. "I have already informed the ministry, and they have ordered you to vacate the site immediately."

James's shoulders dropped. This was it. He was no longer world-renowned Egyptologist James Campbell. Isabella had no doubt painted the picture that he was a misogynist who had used his title and power to take advantage of his student. And I was probably the stupid, gullible girl who had stars in my eyes for my professor in her story.

Mo shot him one more look of disgust before turning away for the tent.

But before James could walk away with what little dignity he had left, Felipe stalked forward. He swung his shoulder back and launched his fist into James's jaw. Screams and gasps echoed around us.

"James," I cried, moving toward him. Angela pulled me back. I tried to pull away from her, but she wouldn't let me go.

James held his jaw in his hand, his eyes never leaving Felipe's hard stare. After a beat, he turned around and flashed me a look so heartbreaking that I nearly died on the spot. "I'm sorry," he said, before casting his eyes away from me and walking toward his car.

I fell into Angela's embrace, sobs rattling my body.

"I'm sorry," I repeated over and over. Sorry for being so careless. Sorry for embarrassing myself. Sorry for ever meeting James Campbell and ruining his life.

Chapter 25

Thirteen unread texts, eight unanswered calls, and three deleted voicemails—or at least, I assumed they had been deleted since my calls weren't being returned.

My fingers hovered over the little phone icon on my screen. I wanted to try one more time. Maybe this would be the lucky attempt that persuaded James to answer.

They said the definition of insanity was doing the same thing over and over again and expecting different results. I was one more phone call away from eating Tide Pods for dinner.

I tossed the phone aside and stretched out on the bed. It had been three days since The Great Revelation at the site, and I had seen more of my hostel room than I had during the entire trip.

The university had sent me the uncomfortable email I'd been expecting, with choice phrases like "immediate suspension," "pending an ethics review," and my all-time favorite, "disciplinary action." Basically, I wasn't permitted on-site until the ministry finished their investigation and issued their findings to the university.

I imagined James's email had been worse. The general tone after James had left the site for good was that he was the one responsible for our indiscretion. Never mind that I'd been a willing participant, most of the team had taken pity on me as if I had been seduced by a predator.

Nothing could have been further from the truth. I was just as guilty as James. We'd both wanted each other, and I resented being made out into some sort of inferior child who had been taken advantage of. The narrative painted me as a naive girl without a brain to think for herself, which pissed me off. No one had been around when James and I were together to witness our chemistry or to see how he worshipped me. Instead, they had all jumped to the conclusion that I was the victim, and my bet was the ministry would adopt the same tone.

I wished James would talk to me. My gut told me that he wasn't taking this too well. His entire career, which he had strived for to gain independence from his horrible family, was completely shattered. He was an Egyptologist, and surely, the ministry would never allow him to set foot in the country again. *What would Oxford say? Would they fire him?*

My head pounded from thinking too hard.

Knock, knock.

"Go away!" I shouted at the door. Angela was the only person I could stand being around, and she would never have knocked before entering.

The door clicked open halfway anyway and Felipe poked his head through. "Can I come in?"

So much for respecting my boundaries. "You're already *in*." I didn't attempt to hide my sarcasm.

His face was solemn as he entered the room, closing the door on his way. "I brought you something to eat." He took a seat on Angela's bed and held out a plate of stuffed zucchinis.

I didn't move to take it from him or offer a polite thank-you like I normally would have. Instead, I just stared at the ceiling with my arms crossed over my chest.

He put the plate on the side table. "You haven't been downstairs in days," he said.

Angela had been bringing me all my meals when the team was at the hostel, and I would go down for lunch when they were all gone. I chose to shower when they were at the dig site so I wouldn't bump into any of them. I didn't have anything to say to anyone, especially Felipe.

"You're still mad at me." His expression showed disappointment, as if he'd expected a warm reception from me.

All he was getting from me was ice. *Ice ice baby*. "Did you just come here to state the obvious?"

"Kitty. Please. I came to apologize for losing my temper at the site."

"You punched him. You punched him *in the face*." There was no way I was letting him dilute what he had done with meaningless words.

Felipe sat forward. "He shouldn't have taken advantage of you. He is...*was* your professor."

I scoffed aloud. Fuck him for assuming the worst, even though James would most likely be fired.

"He didn't take advantage of me. I wanted to be with him."

His holier-than-though expression made me want to throw up. "Yeah, but it was inappropriate. You had to have seen that."

I rubbed my tired eyes. They were all cried out. To the outside world, a man pushing forty with a twenty-one-year-old student would always seem wrong. People would say that he was with me because he had a Leo DiCaprio complex and that I had daddy issues or that I was a gold digger. I wasn't going to begin to dive into the daddy-issues theory for fear of permanently fucking up my psyche, but I was no gold digger. "I don't care. I love him."

My admission caught Felipe off guard. "You could have any guy you wanted. Why him?" His tone neared irritation.

My mouth twisted. "Why do you care so much?" I didn't owe him or anyone an explanation.

"I think he's a shitty guy for risking your reputation like this in public." The disgust on his face was thick.

Why did he care so much about this? I got that it was shocking to him, to everyone. We were friends, but not best friends, and he was worried way more about my *reputation* than Angela was. Something wasn't adding up.

"You knew about us, didn't you?"

He hung his head, keeping his eyes fixed on his shoes. It was all the confirmation I needed.

"Felipe?" I sat up on the bed and leaned forward. "What did you do?"

When he lifted his face, there was guilt written all over it. "I might have sent Isabella into the temple."

"What? Why?" I thought she had strolled in by accident. She had seemed genuinely surprised by what she had seen.

"She didn't know it, but I saw Dr. Campbell enter when I knew you were in there. You two had been inside for a long time together."

My jaw nearly hit the floor. "How did you find out?"

He grimaced as he surrendered the truth. "I saw what happened during Dr. Moore's lecture."

Our in-the-dark flirtation. I had fucking known it from the way that Felipe had looked at me when we'd all met up afterward. It had been fleeting, but even then, he hadn't been able to hide his distaste.

He continued. "And I guess I realized that you two had a *thing* and it bothered me." His fingers twiddled as he spoke.

"But why? I told you that I wasn't interested in a relationship." I had clearly discussed my boundaries with him, so why did he still care so much?

"I accepted that. But seeing you with him...it just did something to me."

All those times when I had thought we were just friends played in my mind. Joking around at the site. Indulging in late-night snacks downstairs when we were starving after working all day. At the club dancing together with his arm around my waist. None of it had been genuine. It had all been one big pissing contest on his part.

"Let me get this straight," I shouted, jabbing my finger at him. "Instead of accepting that I just wanted to be friends, you decided to be vengeful, essentially ruining my chances of graduating?!"

His skin paled at my tongue-lashing. "I didn't mean for you to risk your degree. I just wanted him to leave you alone."

I shot to my feet. "How the fuck did you think this would play out? That Isabella would do your dirty work and snitch on me, and I would just be allowed back on-site to finish my internship like nothing happened?!" My skin felt like it was ready to melt off with how hot my blood ran.

Felipe sat there mute, no longer the good-looking, sweet guy I'd once known. I didn't know the person before me.

I lifted my chin to the ceiling and shut my eyes. All of this was dizzying. "I fucking defended you," I bit out. "James warned me that you had feelings for me, but I denied it. I genuinely thought you were my friend."

I opened my eyes and looked at him. His mouth turned downward at my disappointment.

"I'll always be your friend, Kitty," he offered softly.

But I slashed my hands in the air. "No! I don't want friends who are vindictive and can't respect boundaries."

"I'm so sorry—"

My phone buzzed, interrupting the apology I didn't care to hear.

I grabbed it and unlocked my screen. It was the email I'd been dreading. My stomach hollowed as I opened it.

"The ministry wants to see me tomorrow to discuss my disciplinary action," I said aloud, not that I owed him any explanation.

He shook his head. "I'm really sorry."

I looked at him, fire in my eyes. "Fuck you. Get out of my room." I pointed at the door and refocused my attention on the email, searching for any clues as to what they had in store for me.

He left without protest.

I was barring the fucking door until my flight home.

Chapter 26

What does one wear to a disciplinary meeting at the ministry? Apparently, nothing from Angela Bowman's wardrobe. She had tried to loan me a white fitted turtleneck dress that displayed my belly button through the material. I'd politely refused. This wasn't *Basic Instinct*.

Black. You wear black. In my case, black pants with a black shirt that was buttoned all the way up to my neck. I believed that a woman could wear whatever she wanted, whenever she wanted, but today, I wasn't leaving anything to chance, least of all my attire.

The hallway outside of the boardroom was empty. The plastic chair creaked as I tapped my foot at hummingbird speed against the leg, which echoed against the walls. I was nervous, and the entire floor would hear it.

The tapping also helped to drown out the sound of the board members inside discussing my fate. The voices were deep and there were many of them. It seemed I would be the lucky participant in a not-so-fun, all-male review. Another bro club shouldn't have surprised me; I was the one who was stupid enough to have expected something different. Would it hurt anyone to have a woman on these boards for a change?! *Sheesh.*

I clutched my notebook to my chest, my fingers digging into the spiral wire. I didn't know what to bring with me, and a notebook seemed appropriate. Maybe I could use it to write down all the adjectives they used to describe my "behavior" and make a collage of them afterward to commemorate this failed internship.

The longer I sat there listening to my name uttered through the walls, the hotter my skin grew from embarrassment, and the more my stomach churned like I had just drunk a twenty-four-ounce Nitro Brew on an empty stomach. *Barf.*

Footsteps echoed down the hall, and my foot fell still from its tapping. Expensive male shoes captured my attention, and I let my gaze travel up to find their owner.

"James," I gasped.

Our eyes locked, but his weren't the lively blue I was used to seeing when they looked at me. These before me were tired and dull. His whole face looked exhausted, from the bags that hollowed out his eyes to his unshaven jaw, covered in thick stubble—the most I had ever seen on him. Yet, somehow, he had still managed to dress impeccably in a gray suit with a navy tie.

"Sanura." His voice was hoarse as he held my gaze, studying my face as if he were seeing me for the first time. Like he had forgotten me.

My mouth opened, but I couldn't find the right words. He had ghosted me. After that horrible day at the site, I had just wanted to know he was alright, and he'd left me hanging. He hadn't bothered to check on me. How about how I was? Did I not matter enough to him to reach out?

"I-I didn't know you'd be here."

"Neither did I." He took the seat across from me. Navy-blue and gray argyle-patterned socks were on display under the cuffs of his pants.

The ministry had been very discreet in their email, so I didn't know what—or *whom*—to expect.

He propped his leg up on his knee and clasped his fingers over it. His frame was too tall for the chair, but he managed to sit in it with his spine tall and his elbows flared, never compromising his stature for the chair's shortcomings.

My cheeks heated under his stare, though they shouldn't have. He'd made it clear that we were over. It was better for the both of us if I moved on...fast.

We sat in painful silence for some time. Every minute felt like an hour. Occasionally, I'd turn to check the doorway, hoping that someone would call for me. Yeah, I was desperate enough that I'd rather be eviscerated by some man with small-dick syndrome than sit with James in silence for another moment longer.

He licked his lips, running his tongue along the bottom slowly, and I cursed myself for watching—for being hypnotized. *Old habits die hard.* He started, "Sanura, I—"

Suddenly, the door to the boardroom swung open and a tall man with a full head of dark hair emerged. "Dr. Campbell. Ms. Taha. Please, come in."

A two-for-one hanging. *Lovely.*

James held out his hand, signaling me to pass first. I padded through the door into the spacious room. It was more like a courtroom than a boardroom, with a long desk at the far end and each of its eight spots occupied by a man in a suit. Each minister came in different flavors: dark-haired, graying, semi-bald, and bald. *Collect 'em all.*

I recognized the man in the middle with thinning gray hair and a slim build. He was the man from the site, the one who'd given James a migraine.

The name plate before him read "Mahmoud Emara, Minister of State." *Shit.* He was the head of the ministry.

I'd known this was bad, but it had just gotten a whole lot worse. I was going to jail today, just as I had promised Mom I wouldn't do.

There were no seats available for us in front of the polished wooden pulpit, so I stood on wobbly knees, clinging to my notebook. I was about two seconds away from pulling my pen from my pocket and clicking away my anxiety.

James stood next to me, hands clasped in front of him, waiting for the board to begin. He seemed oddly at ease. Not comfortable like he was at a spa getting a massage, but more like a robot. No emotions, just existing—waiting for the next command—so unlike the fiery man I had met in the desert nearly eight weeks ago.

Mr. Emara shuffled some papers on the table and read through them through his thin-framed glasses. He took the frames off and rested one arm's end against his lips as he peered down at James. "Dr. Campbell, are you aware of why you are here today?"

James's chest puffed out at attention. "Yes, sir."

Mr. Emara waved him on. "Tell me in your own words what happened."

Oh, God, he was going to make us say it out loud. This couldn't get any more mortifying. Maybe if I passed out, they'd skip my turn!

"I had inappropriate relations with a student." James's voice rang clearly through my ears, his words slicing my heart in half.

Inappropriate relations. He'd said it just as it would be written in my academic file for the rest of my life. Like a sordid affair driven by hormones, not something that we had felt in our hearts—in our souls.

I wanted to cry.

Mr. Emara nodded. "According to the code of conduct, this is a direct violation. You understand that?"

"I do," James acknowledged plainly.

"The most appropriate course of action would be to strip you of your grant for the remainder of the current season, and you must relinquish all rights to your research on the temple. You are no longer a mentor in this internship program, nor will you be permitted to be one in the future."

James's face remained blank, like he had already anticipated this.

Mr. Emara continued, "You will be suspended from excavations in Egypt until further notice. I am certain Oxford will have some words for you as well when you return home."

My chest squeezed so tight, threatening to cut off the air supply to my lungs. Why was I the only one panicking here?! This was James's career. They were halting his work on the temple and stripping him of his research, yet he was ready to give it up so easily, without a fight? It didn't make sense.

I silently pleaded for him to do something—anything—other than stand there like a puppet.

As if reading my thoughts, he shook his head at me, as if to warn me against exploding.

But I couldn't stay quiet. I'd defend him if he wasn't going to do it for himself. I couldn't stand by and let such a brilliant mind to go to waste. His career was everything to him, and one day, when this zombie-like state wore off, he'd regret not fighting for it.

"No! You can't do that!" I shouted, taking Mr. Emara by surprise.

The rest of the board muttered uneasily.

"You don't accept our decision, Ms. Taha?" The edge in Mr. Emara's voice should have frightened me, but I had officially lost all sanity with my outburst.

"James—I mean...Dr. Campbell did nothing wrong." My hands flailed emphatically, notebook still in my grasp.

Mr. Emara's voice hardened. "Ms. Taha, you engaged in a lewd relationship with your professor. Both of you were wrong. Your behavior reflects directly on this ministry, and because of this, I have no choice but to recommend to your university that you be expelled from your degree program."

My stomach dropped. I was getting kicked out of Stanford. A recommendation from the ministry would almost certainly convince the dean to expel me.

Like a knife, James's voice sliced through the chaos. "No, you won't."

"Excuse me?" Mr. Emara's eyes widened, red capillaries visible from strain.

"You're not going to say anything to her university."

Mr. Emara's body stiffened. He didn't seem like the type who was used to being ordered around. "I am not debating this with you, James. This *girl* clearly lacks the judgment needed to represent this ministry and her university."

I grimaced at the condescension.

James approached the bench, his strides slow and purposeful like a snake ready to strike at the right moment. "You do whatever you want to me, but you'll leave her alone." His voice was sinister with warning.

Mr. Emara stood, planting his hands on the table. "I'm afraid we've all voted, and this is our decision."

"Fuck your vote," James growled.

"James!" I gasped, forgetting all formalities in front of the board.

Mr. Emara huffed out a breath. "Dr. Campbell," the minister warned, standing over James. "You need to get a hold of yourself. You're lucky I haven't thrown you both in jail for indecency yet."

James ignored him as if he hadn't spoken at all. "You're going to let her go home and you won't say anything to the university."

Mr. Emara, clearly losing his patience, pinned his white-knuckled fists to his hips. "And why is that?"

James turned to look at me, his face softening. "Because this woman is brilliant."

The minister scoffed, and his back-up singers snickered in tune. "She's just a girl. A silly girl who has hearts in her eyes for someone like you who can advance her career."

His insult stung my chest. I could feel tears burning my eyes, and I looked to my shoes to hide them. I wanted to run and hide and never see the light of day again. It shouldn't be this hard being a woman.

"Don't talk about the woman I love like that."

My head snapped up to find James's piercing gaze on me. *Love.* That single word instantly pulled me out of my impending spiral into darkness, bringing me back to the present—to what was before me. Did James really love me?

"Yes, love," he confirmed to Mr. Emara. Even though I had heard it with my ears, I couldn't believe it. He could have just used the love-card to garner sympathy from the board—to convince them to lighten their sentence for me.

"She is anything but a weak and petty child," James continued. "Ms. Taha is the brightest and most driven student I have ever mentored. You'd do good to realize that she's an asset to you."

Mr. Emara's mouth twisted in disgust. "I highly doubt that *she* is worth anything to us."

"She has what you want."

The minister's brow furrowed. "What is that?"

Even I was confused as fuck. I was still stuck on the part where James might or might not love me.

James leaned over the desk. "A discovery," he said, so low that it was almost a whisper.

Gasps sounded from the rest of the board. Mr. Emara stood dumbstruck, unsure of how to proceed.

I wracked my brain, trying to figure out what he was talking about. *The cartouche!* I had completely forgotten about it through everything. James had taken it with him, and it appeared that he'd never reported it, either. If I hadn't been on the chopping block for unethical behavior, I would totally have laid into him about keeping the find a secret for days.

"What is this discovery?" Mr. Emara demanded.

"You'll have to ask her. Drop her punishment and you'll find out." James looked back at me, flashing me a quick wink. So, this was why he had been so calm. He'd already had a plan. I sank my teeth into my lip to keep myself from smiling like a lunatic. James Campbell had once again proved himself to be a genius.

Mr. Emara slammed his fist into the desk, the thud startling everyone except for James, puppet-master extraordinaire. "Tell us or we'll sue you."

"Actually, you can't." I stepped forward, carefully. My voice wavered, but I continued. "The fine print on my attestation says that I am the sole responsibility of my mentor and any discoveries that I should make during my internship will be under the blanket of my mentor's own research. And since you've already fired him, he will not be able to hand his intern's discovery off to the ministry, since it was never recorded and catalogued in the first place. There is no evidence that it even exists, especially since neither of us are permitted to return to the site to share it with anyone. I have nothing to share with you as an *ex*-intern."

Mom always says, "Read contracts!"

The ministers looked at one another, their unease showing.

"How do I know you're not lying about this discovery?" It was clear Mr. Emara hated that he'd been reduced to bartering with someone he found so insignificant.

I approached the bench, courage coursing through my veins. I placed my hand on the edge of the table, standing next to James. His warmth was all the encouragement I needed. "If I'm lying, then you can throw me in jail."

The minister's jaw clenched, as if I were tempting him to do that very thing. But then his eyes caught on James's snarling glare.

"Throw her in jail and you'll regret it."

Mr. Emara's Adam's apple bobbed. "Fine, I'll rescind my recommendation to the university."

It wasn't enough for me. "What about him?" My head tilted in James's direction. Peripherally, I saw he was holding back a smile. He was loving my negotiation skills.

"What about him?" Mr. Emara huffed.

"You'll give him back his title and grant," I ordered, pinning each of the men in turn with my gaze. I wouldn't budge on this.

But Mr. Emara was resistant. "I can't do tha—"

I stopped him. "Try again. I'm not sharing anything with you until you restore his title."

Like a cat backed into a corner, Mr. Emara nervously glanced left and right to his board members.

After a moment, he spoke. "Please wait outside while we discuss this."

Adrenaline coursed through me. This might actually have worked! I wanted to laugh hysterically and cry all at the same time from the high I was riding.

James ushered me outside.

As soon as the door clicked closed, I tossed my notebook onto a chair and swung around to face James. "Oh, my God!" I mouthed.

He responded with a quiet chuckle. That brightness had returned to his blue eyes from all the excitement. His plan had been brilliant, and the fact that we were out here waiting in the hall had to be a good sign.

"I really think they'll cave," I said.

He slipped his hands into his pockets. "They have no choice. They know if I'm claiming to have found something, it must be significant."

"Where is the cartouche now?"

"It's at home in my safe which has temperature and moisture controls."

I giggled. "That's very *you*."

He tilted his head to one side, his long locks swaying with the movement. My fingers tingled remembering how silky they felt. "What do you mean?"

"You're smart and you'd think to place it somewhere secure like a tricked out safe."

"You're smart, too. The way you so effortlessly brought up that part about the attestation. Beautiful."

My cheeks felt hot, though the word had been meant for my action and not me. "I like to read contracts." I tried to shrug it off, but I was sure he saw the faint blush of red my skin tone would allow. "What if we're wrong about our theory?"

It was possible that the cartouche was a fake to disguise the real patron.

"We're not," James answered plainly.

His confidence baffled me. He seemed so sure with only one piece of evidence.

"Why do you say that?"

"Because the lab results came back from the bracelet you found."

The one made of lapis lazuli with the flower clasp.

I wet my lips. The tip of my tongue caught his stare. "And?"

He cleared his throat and met my eyes once again. "Funny thing. X-ray fluorescence found that the iron clasp had high levels of nickel. It contained cobalt, too."

"What does that mean?"

"It was made from iron meteorite."

Extraterrestrial rock from outer space. There was only one other item that I knew that had been made from a meteorite. "The dagger," I whispered in disbelief. It was the burial dagger found in Tutankhamun's tomb. Scientists had run tests and found that it was comprised of levels of nickel higher than in any other iron found on Earth.

James nodded. "It appears the bracelet and Tutankhamun's dagger were fashioned from the same material."

My mind raced. This meant that the bracelet had most likely belonged to someone of great importance, just like Tutankhamun. Like his wife, Ankhesenamun. "It's *hers*."

"My guess is she also visited the temple herself to honor her dead husband and offered the bracelet to the gods on his behalf. She had probably been banned from ever visiting Tutankhamun's mortuary temple, wherever it is, by Ay if she was married to him after Tut's death. Perhaps she built this temple so she could continue to honor her fallen pharaoh in private. This would explain why it wasn't lavish like a mortuary temple."

I was completely stunned. Tutankhamun's mortuary temple had yet to be discovered, but this temple was definitely not it. Mortuary temples were grand and ostentatious just like the pharaohs who commissioned them. It was too small and too humble to be his official death temple.

My theory was right. A woman had commissioned the temple. Ankhese-namun had wanted to honor the love she had for her husband, to have his memory live on forever. I wanted to shout for joy.

"Are you going to tell the minister when he calls us back inside?"

James shook his head. "You will. It's *your* discovery."

I beamed. *My discovery.* I couldn't believe that I was the one who had made such an amazing revelation. Mom would lose her shit when I told her.

My smile faded and silence filled the space between us. I looked down at my fingers, knotted together before me.

There was something else I'd remembered. *He loved me.* Were his words true? I wouldn't be able to handle it if they weren't. *I should probably just leave the topic alone until he brings it up again . . .*

Before I could decide my next step, he spoke. "I meant it."

My heart stopped. I looked up. "What?"

He stepped closer. "I meant all of it." His eyes bore into mine, our souls connecting. "Kitten, I love you."

My core melted at his intoxicating words.

"But...you ghosted me," I breathed out. "I thought we were over."

His chin tipped lower, his breath warm on my face. "I'm sorry. Can you ever forgive me? I hated myself for risking your career, and I thought it was best to leave you alone before I ruined any more of your life."

I wanted so badly to grab onto his neck, to run my fingers down his chest and feel his heartbeat under my touch. "It wasn't your fault. I was re-sponsible, too."

"I'm your mentor and I'm responsible for your educational well-being and I shouldn't have jeopardized your career."

"*Were*...you were my mentor," I corrected, reminding him that he could be free of any guilt he carried.

"That's right. *Were.*" He drew in closer, his scent of books and whiskey surrounding me. I closed my eyes, savoring the aroma. "When everything happened, I should have checked on you. I should have made sure you were alright, but I felt like your life would be better if I left for good."

"James, we're in this together. Both of our careers were at stake, and I just wanted to know that you were okay."

A meek smile spread across his lips. "I am now."

"I tried to tell you before Isabella found us, but then all hell broke loose. I love you, too."

Without hesitating, he pressed his lips to mine, breathing life into me again. Our mouths fit perfectly together as if we were two pieces of a puzzle, completing the part that had been missing since he'd walked away.

As quickly as our reunion had started, it ended. He pulled away from me, and my lips mourned the loss.

The door suddenly opened, and the minister stepped into the hall. He studied us, skepticism etched on his brow, but whatever he had been thinking was swiftly dismissed. "We have reached a decision. Please enter."

We re-entered the room to face our fate. Whatever it was, we would be okay because we had each other.

Chapter 27

Five months later

My fingers tapped on the keyboard, the rhythm matching the second hand's ticks on the clock mounted next to me.

Tap tap tap. Tick tick tick.

The tune must have been infectious because even the cursor on the screen blinked on beat.

I waited for that *Aha!* moment to strike—the one where hundreds of figurative light bulbs would illuminate simultaneously to frame the one idea that was *it*. But inspiration was hard to come by these days. I was too distracted.

The house was too quiet. I missed the sound of Mom rummaging through the kitchen for snacks, or Angela dropping by unexpectedly to lure me to an *emergency* sale at the mall.

I was all alone. It should have been a good thing because I needed to focus. I wasn't yet used to having much free time on my hands and often found myself wasting whole days just in time for my anxiety to rage when I got into bed and remind me of my deadlines.

I could feel a migraine coming on, the all-too-familiar pressure crushing my forehead. They had been frequent visitors the last month, and I was pretty sure I was starting to develop a tolerance to over-the-counter pain relievers.

I pulled out my tightly wound hair-tie and let my curly tresses cascade over my shoulders. Digging my nails into my scalp, I tried to massage out some of the tension.

A break was needed since I wasn't getting anywhere with my task. I pulled my phone out and scrolled through Instagram. A notification came up with a memory from May. *The internship.*

It was one we had taken after our first day. All five of us were all covered in dust, but we had the biggest smiles on our faces. Even Isabella looked like she'd been having the time of her life. Who knew you could look so fulfilled from shoveling sand?!

My smile stretched so wide in the photo that I could feel my jaw aching as I took in every detail of my face. Everything had been new and exciting that day, as if we w about to uncover the discovery of our lives even though I had sorted pottery pieces for three hours.

My heart twisted remembering how close we had been at the beginning. We had shared a bond that one would only know if they had spent two months in a foreign country working on an excavation site for the first time.

Sean's smile caught my eye. He'd gone back to England after the internship and was currently in his last year. Luckily but not surprisingly, he had been accepted into graduate school at Cambridge and would be starting his PhD next fall.

I still kept in touch with him sometimes, but I knew that he talked to Angela way more often than she admitted. She had been so cagey when I had asked her what she planned to do during her London vacation over winter break. Instead, I should have asked *who* she planned to do.

As for Isabella...well...we didn't speak. I had never really been able to connect with her other than that night we'd spent together for her birthday. After everything had blown up when she'd found out about James and me, she'd grown cold. She had judged me for sleeping with the boss, but I couldn't fault her for that. It was only natural to be critical when you didn't have all of the facts.

Regardless of her opinions, I wished her well. Sean had said that she was currently on track to graduate with full honors and had been accepted to apprentice under the Ministry of Antiquities in Peru.

Aside from spending holidays with Sean, Angela was only a semester away from graduation. According to her GPA, she ranked at the top of the graduating Stanford archaeology class, and I could not have been more proud of her. She hadn't received her acceptance letter yet, but she was hoping to join Sean in Cambridge for graduate school.

I noticed the owner of the arm around my shoulders in the photo. *Felipe.* After all this time, my stomach still squeezed with disappointment when I thought of him. I'd thought our friendship had been real, but sometimes things were just not as they appeared to be. We hadn't kept in touch after the internship. He had sent a few emails, but I hadn't opened any of them. I couldn't move past the deceit. I wished things had ended differently, but I couldn't forgive him for setting Isabella up to catch James and me.

Angela had heard through Sean that Felipe was thriving in school and that he had applied to be a part of an excavation team in Pompeii. I hoped he was selected, even if we weren't friends anymore.

My eyes fixated on the final figure. He wasn't the center of the photo, but he was suddenly all I could focus on. *James.* With his arms crossed over his chest and a circle of crewmen around him, he popped out of the background like a star in the night sky. He had most likely been issuing orders that he'd have expected to be carried out at lightning speed. His brow was furrowed in the image, just like it always was at work. The stubble on his jaw was thick enough to give him that sexy five o'clock shadow any time of day. My mouth watered at the way the fabric of his shirt stretched across his broad chest. I could remember how it had felt to touch his bare pecs for the first time—smooth skin over hard rock. And his scent, it always reminded me of the books in his office mixed with liquor.

A loud click sounded down the hall. I turned in my seat to look out the door to see what it was. "Hello?" I called out, but no one answered. I had set the alarm on the front door—or at least, I thought I had. It was probably nothing. I turned back around to face my laptop, which was on the desk against the window.

Suddenly, red flashed before my eyes, and I nearly jumped out of my seat.

The object became clear. *A rose.*

I clutched at my chest, trying to catch my breath, eyes traveling down the stem and up the arm that held it.

"Aren't you supposed to be working?" James asked, his thick fingers holding onto the stem as if it were fragile.

"I am." I yanked the rose from his grasp and sniffed its floral sweetness before placing it on the desk. Little gestures like this always set the butterflies in my belly to vibrating.

"*Instagram Memories* is work?" he teased, eyeing my screen.

"You revisit the past every day, but when I do it, I'm slacking off?"

"Those are your words. Not mine." He leaned over me, his boozy book scent enveloping me, as he examined the photo. "I remember that day."

"Oh, yeah?"

He chuckled. "You seemed so uncomfortable when I was going over my expectations for the internship."

"Well, yeah! It was hot as Hades and I was wearing clothes that were two sizes too small for me." I shuddered at the memory of shoving myself into Angela's micro-wardrobe while my suitcase was lost.

"That's not why." He bent over, his face hovering over mine. I couldn't have missed the way he looked at my bottom lip, like he was hungry for a taste. He pulled at it with his thumb. "This lip was trembling when I first addressed you. I made you nervous," he said, his voice gravelly like he was about to own me.

I puckered my lips, anticipating him closing the space and pressing his mouth against mine. But he pulled away, his cheeky grin teasing me.

Instead of mourning the loss, I smacked his bicep. "Have *you* ever worked for you?!"

"I'm not that bad."

"Excuse me?!" I had to do a double take to make sure I had heard him correctly. "You're clearly delusional!"

He shook his head. Denial was clearly not just a river in Egypt, or whatever that joke was. "I'll have you know that my crew has no complaints."

I laughed so emphatically that it came out as a snort. "Yeah, because if they did, they'd never work in this town again," I said, mimicking his British accent. "I thought you were going to be gone all afternoon? Did the ministry get sick of you or something?"

"As if they could ever do without me. They need me." He had a hell of an ego on him, but I supposed that made him even sexier—that and his fat dick. "We finished up early. They just had a few more questions about our research at the temple."

James had been working overtime wrapping up his work on the temple. He was at the Luxor Museum almost daily, working with museum curators to properly catalog and organize all artifacts, photos, and notes taken during the excavation. The ministry had been all over him to make sure that his final report was complete before publishing to secure wealthy donors with deep pockets to help in the preservation of the temple. The board combed over every draft only to chuck more corrections at him.

But still, their attitude toward James now was a far cry from how they had treated him when they'd found out about our relationship.

After deliberating over our punishment, Mr. Emara, the head of the ministry, had called James and me back into the boardroom with his tail tucked between his legs. James had been permitted to resume his research in exchange for a detailed account of our finding—Ankhesenamun's cartouche. The board had been flabbergasted when I'd finally shared my discovery. James had informed them of the composition analysis of the bracelet that I had also found and how it seemed to have been made from the same meteorite material as Tutankhamun's burial dagger.

Overcome with excitement, the ministry had immediately extended James's dig permit to continue work at the site for another month even though the summer heat had already become unbearable. They had also doubled the size of his crew to help excavate deeper under the ground. The ministry was desperate to continue with the project.

James had gone straight back to work after being re-hired and had ended up uncovering what appeared to be a workshop adjacent to the temple. It seemed that Ankhesenamun had hired an entire team of artisans, scribes, and priests to create gifts and offerings to the gods in her husband's honor.

It was the first temple to be uncovered that had been commissioned by the wife of a pharaoh to honor her husband.

As for me, Mr. Emara had completely pretended that he hadn't berated me like a child in front of the board. Instead, he'd fawned over my discovery and theory that Ankhesenamun was the true patron of the temple. I had been permitted to continue the tail end of my internship without any word getting back to Stanford about my relationship with James.

I had extended my stay for another month after the internship ended to continue working alongside James. Honestly, it had felt liberating to be with him and not have to worry about keeping it a secret. Although we still hadn't shown affection in public, the crew had known that we were together but never said much of anything about it. The initial shock had worn off and almost everyone had accepted it, even Mo.

I had come clean about everything to Mom when I'd told her I would be staying in Egypt for another month. She hadn't been very happy with me hooking up with my professor, but I had convinced her that the relationship was deeper than it might have seemed on the surface. She'd been a bit wary of me spending more time away, especially knowing I'd be with James.

James had been serious when he'd said he loved me. He had refused to let me stay at the hostel another moment longer and had moved me and all my things into his house, where I'd stayed until the end of the dig. We had immediately fallen into a comfortable relationship: work all day, then come home and shower, eat dinner together, and curl up in bed with a movie until we couldn't keep our eyes open any longer.

Sex had been a morning event for us. Like clockwork, I'd been awakened to the feeling of James's weight on me. Some mornings, he hadn't waited until I woke up; I'd just come to with his cock between my legs.

The man was insatiable, and I was drunk off him.

After the dig was over, I'd flown back home, and he'd had to return to England. My heart had ached from the separation. Keeping in touch had proved to be a challenge, too, with the time change and his crazy work hours, but somehow, we had made it work. I'd visited him once in the fall and had gotten to see where he lived and where he worked. The library in Oxford was ideal for finger-banging, if anyone was curious.

When James had suggested I visit him over winter break, I'd jumped at the chance to come back to Egypt with him. As soon as we had crossed the threshold, it had been like no time had passed between us.

It had been blissful so far. The lust and passion for each other was still there, as was the ease of being together. I could see myself being with him forever, though I feared it was premature to be making that observation. A semester and my capstone project still stood in the way of graduation. I was far too busy to be thinking about marrying James Campbell and having little archaeologist babies of our own with golden-blond hair and blue eyes. Much too busy.

And who's to say that James even wanted to settle down at all? There was a little more than a fifteen-year age gap between us, and if he hadn't thought about marriage with anyone else by now, then maybe it was off the table for him.

James leaned against the desk and nodded to my laptop. "Any luck while I was gone?"

I tossed my phone aside and heaved out a huge sigh, rubbing my palms into my eyes to wipe away the tiredness. "None. Thanks for letting me borrow your office to work, but it was a complete waste of time."

The office in his Egyptian penthouse was massive. It boasted the most comfortable leather desk chair my ass had ever had the pleasure of sitting on, and the shine on his mahogany desk rivaled the best car buff I had ever seen. I would have had a better time taking a nap in here rather than straining my brain.

James took my hands in his big ones and pulled me up. Trading places with me, he patted his lap, gesturing for me to sit.

I did as he asked, feeling his warm thighs under my legs.

He assumed control over the mouse pad on my device, his arm caging me in as his fingers glided around. I could feel his breath on my neck as he scanned my edits.

For my capstone project, I'd written a research paper on my theory about Ankhesenamun building the temple for Tutankhamun. I'd included all the findings from the dig that supported my statement. James had been helpful by filling in the holes from the beginning of the project, which had taken place the year before I'd arrived for the internship.

"The paper looks complete," he said.

"Oh, thank God." I huffed out an exasperated breath.

He kept scrolling. "Except...where's the title?"

Oh, yeah—the thing that I'd been wracking my brain over for the last hour. "Um...that's what I'm stuck on." I flashed him a toothy grin, hoping any sort of cuteness would distract him from further nagging.

But it was a failure. "You didn't name your paper yet?" he prodded.

I tilted my head back on his shoulder and stared up at the ceiling. "You make it sound like it should be so easy. This is my capstone. The project that earns me my degree. How can I possibly settle on a title when we found so many things that were equally relevant?"

He nudged me to cease the theatrics and to sit upright. It was his way of saying, *We have shit to accomplish.* "You're thinking too hard and it's fucking with your brain. This is the last step you need to complete before submitting your paper to your adviser for proofing. Is it possible that the finality of it all is holding you back?"

I hadn't thought about it that way. Maybe I was sabotaging myself because this was essentially the last big obstacle standing in the way of me earning my degree. "Maybe," I grunted with my arms crossed over my chest.

He pulled my hair aside, exposing my neck. His warm lips pressed a soft kiss just below my ear, bringing my skin to life. "What is your paper about?"

I rolled my eyes. "You know what it's about."

"This isn't for me. It's for you to brainstorm effectively. Tell me what it's about."

His strategy sounded stupid, but I wasn't getting anywhere doing it my way, so it couldn't hurt to try another way. "It's about findings at the temple that—"

He cut me off. "No. Not all of that. Don't list each find. What was the result of your research, in one word?"

I exhaled forcefully as my brain worked. "Um...a discovery?"

James's brow hitched and his voice deepened. "Are you asking me or telling me?"

Ugh. I hated when he got all teacher on me. Okay, I didn't hate it all the time. It was still fun to role-play in the bedroom sometimes.

"A discovery happened," I said firmly.

"Good," he nodded. "A discovery of what?"

"Dusty swag belonging to dead people?"

"Sanura," he warned.

My first name on his lips in that tone made my thighs squeeze together.

"What did you find in the temple? The bigger idea. Maybe it was something intangible, like a concept."

I thought about what concept I had stumbled upon during my internship. "Love."

"Love?" he asked with interest.

"Yeah...love. Ankhesenamun built the temple out of love for Tutankhamun, to honor him for eternity. As fucked up as it was that she was also his sister, there was something beautiful about her loyalty to Tutankhamun. She covertly created the temple, though it was modest, behind everyone's back as a testament to her determination. We should all be so lucky to find someone who loves us the way that Ankhesenamun loved Tutankhamun."

I could see my words marinating in his mind. "It's definitely intriguing. What other key words jump out at you that belong in the title?"

Before I could answer, my phone rang.

I looked at the screen. "Aaqil?"

James peeked over my shoulder at the name on the caller ID. "The PI?"

"Yeah." I hadn't heard from him in months. He seemed to have run into a dead end while searching for my uncle and his family. I'd been a complete mess after that last phone call and it had taken me two days to snap out of my depression.

I had forced myself to come to terms with the fact that I would never meet my dad's brother. Baba was long gone, as were any remnants of his past. It was time for me to move on.

"Answer it," James urged when I just stared at the screen like an idiot.

Unwanted feelings bubbled inside me as I pressed the phone icon. "Hello?"

The curt voice on the other end responded, "Hello? Miss Sanura?"

"Yes. Hi, Aaqil. How are you?"

"Do you have a pen and paper nearby?" he asked abruptly.

"Uh—what—yes. I do." I put the phone between my ear and shoulder and grabbed the notepad and pen from the desk, all the while waiting for him to explain why I needed them.

"I have an address. You'll want to write it down."

My eyes widened as Aaqil rattled off the information at warp speed. My brain, and hand, could barely keep up with his words.

James stared at me with concern. "What?" he mouthed.

I covered the mouthpiece, my pulse racing. "We need to leave for London."

Chapter 28

"Are you sure you want me to go in? It might seem inappropriate that I'm here with you."

The man who was my boyfriend and not my husband. I didn't care about any cultural conventions that his presence would break. I gripped James's hand tighter, my nails digging into his flesh. "If you don't come with me, I don't think I can do this."

"I'm here," he whispered. His thumb stroked my knuckles, taming some of my anxiety.

I lifted my chin and steeled my spine. *One last deep breath.* Then I pressed the doorbell.

I could hear the faint chime from the other side of the dark brown door.

Moments felt like hours.

"Do you think he's home?" James asked.

"He said he would be when I called last night."

After the shock had worn off from Aaqil's call, I had somehow mustered enough courage to call the number that he had given for my uncle. As if the universe were rooting me on, a man had answered on the second ring.

His voice was surreal yet familiar—the same slightly hoarse airiness in it that Baba had in home videos.

We'd talked for an hour and a half. Apparently, he hadn't known how to contact me since Mom and I had moved shortly after Baba had passed away. Back then, my uncle hadn't spoken any English, so all his communication had been solely through Baba. He had learned English since then because we could both understand each other during our conversation.

He and his wife, my aunt Miriam, had sold their business and moved to England years ago to join my cousins, Shireen and Shiraz, who were attending university in London. The entire family had been living there ever since.

Uncle Yusuf was very eager to meet, so I'd followed my heart after hanging up with him and booked the first flight to London that I could find for myself and James. It had been impulsive, but I couldn't wait any longer.

I rang the bell and listened to it chime again. A shadow darkened the stained-glass flower design in the center of the door.

It opened, revealing a little boy with wavy dark hair and matching brown eyes, no older than nine years old, standing with his hand on his hip.

I looked to James, unsure of how to proceed since I'd been expecting someone over five feet to answer, but he just shrugged his shoulders. "Um...hi. I'm Sanura."

"I'm Samir." He offered a quick wave but nothing more.

"Is there an adult at home?"

He narrowed his eyes at me before turning his head and calling out into the house, "Baba! Some weird lady is here."

James chuckled next to me.

Suddenly, a man approached the boy and rested his hands on his shoulders. He had to be in his late fifties, with salt-and-pepper hair on his head and chin. His eyes were dark just like mine but with wrinkles around the corners. He looked so much like photos of my Baba.

"I...um . . ." I was at a loss for words. All these years I had spent dreaming of this very moment when I'd meet my dad's family, imagining what I would say, what I would do...And now that it was actually happening, my mind was paralyzed.

James came to my rescue. "Hello, I am James Campbell. And this is my girlfriend, S—"

"Sanura," the man whispered. He studied my face, registering all the commonalities we shared just as I had. "Is that really you?"

I nodded. "Yes." Mist clouded my eyes, but there was no mistaking the glassiness that had overtaken his, too.

"You look so much like Babu," he breathed out.

Babu. My father's nickname. My mother always referred to him as Babu whenever we spoke about him at home.

The little boy looked up at my uncle expectantly. "Baba, who is she?" When we had spoken on the phone, my uncle had only mentioned my cousins as his "children." I had just assumed there were only the two who were adults, whom the PI had confirmed months ago. I was surprised to see that he had a third child, who was so young in comparison to the others.

"Samir, this is your cousin, Sanura."

Samir's small mouth fixed into a frown. "I didn't know I had any cousins."

I kneeled down to his level, meeting his innocent eyes. "Neither did I. Well, not until a few months ago."

He was quiet for a moment. I could see the wheels turning in his head. Whatever had had him thinking so hard was suddenly forgotten. "Are you going to stay to play? I have a cool Bakugan set. We can battle each other."

My smile was honest and true. "I'd love to play." I had no idea what the fuck a Bakugan was, but I was willing to find out if it meant I could spend time with my cousin.

Samir pulled on the hem of his dad's shirt. "Baba, can she stay?"

My uncle laughed, and a single tear trailed down his cheek. "Yes. Come in, Sanura and James."

We removed our shoes and followed my uncle, and he introduced us to his wife, who had cooked a lavish dinner for us. For the next three hours, we talked nonstop, making up for lost time.

Uncle Yusuf told me all about my other cousins who also lived in London. Shiraz was a chemical engineer for the government, and Shireen was a doctor. Shireen was already married, while Shiraz was engaged to be married in spring.

He showed me albums full of photos of Baba from their childhood and shared endless stories about their adventures. I found out that Baba had had an interest in archaeology, too, and had read as many *National Geographic* magazines as he could get his hands on. It warmed me to think that if he had still been alive, he probably would have loved to visit my dig site.

James wasn't deprived of attention, either. Uncle Yusuf and Aunt Miriam adored him. They asked plenty of questions about his career and research. If they thought it awkward that I was with a man I wasn't married to, they never showed it. And Samir was perhaps the most smitten with him. Watching the two of them sit on the floor and battle with Bakugans, which I found out were these little magnetic balls that exploded into crazy shapes, was the sweetest thing ever. James was a natural with kids, and my uterus noticed.

Just when my face started to cramp up from all the smiling, Samir let out a huge yawn, which was our signal that the family reunion was over.

Uncle Yusuf walked James and me to the door. My hands were full with foil-covered paper plates that had been packed by Aunt Miriam. She'd insisted we take food home in case we were hungry later.

We slipped our shoes on and stepped out onto the porch.

"How long are you staying in London?" Uncle Yusuf asked.

"We leave tomorrow." The flight here had been spur of the moment; James and I needed to get back to Egypt to wrap up our research. But I hadn't thought about how it would feel to say goodbye to the family I had just found.

"Do you know when you'll be in London again?"

James had a home, or rather a mini-mansion, in Oxford that we were staying in now, but after the new year, I wouldn't have another break until spring. And I would most likely be busy during spring break preparing to present my capstone project.

"I'm not sure."

Uncle Yusuf's face fell. I felt his pain, too. To have found each other only to separate again without knowing when we'd be reunited seemed like a cruel plot twist.

I attempted to lighten his mood. "But you have my phone number, and we can always FaceTime. Or email. Email works, too!" I was poking around in the dark to find anything that would wipe the sadness off his face.

"Don't worry about me, Sanura. I may have lost my brother, but I will make sure I never lose you again. We're family, and that means we are always bonded together, even when we are apart." He rested his hand to his heart.

My own heart felt full hearing his words. I couldn't help but think that Baba was somewhere looking down on us and smiling, too.

We hugged and parted ways. James and I walked to his car, the sound of our shoes clicking on the driveway. I pulled my coat tighter. The air was a lot colder than it had been when we had arrived.

The tears started. I couldn't fight the sniffles that perforated the night air.

James wrapped his arm around my shoulders, pulling me into his warmth. "Are you okay, kitten?" he asked.

I turned into his body, releasing my sobs into his chest. "I barely know them, but it feels like I've lost them all over again. All this time wasted. And now I have to leave them behind."

He rubbed slow circles on my back. "Do you want to stay longer? We could extend our ticket."

I pulled back and shook my head. "No. You have to meet with the ministry again the day after our flight, and I need to finish my draft." I hadn't packed my laptop in my haste to get to the airport in time to board.

"You'll be back. After graduation, you can come back and spend the summer with them."

It felt too far away. I wanted to meet Shiraz and Shireen. I wanted to play with Samir and learn recipes from Aunt Miriam.

James pulled me back into his chest, allowing me to cry for as long as I needed. "I wish there were instructions or some shit on how to deal with this stuff," I blubbered out.

"What stuff?"

"The curveballs that life throws at you."

His chin rested atop my head. "That would be nice. Like some sort of algorithm to get you through difficult situations."

"There's so much emphasis on going to school, finding a good job, and getting married that you would think that was all you needed to set you up for happiness."

"But it's never that easy. That formula is severely lacking."

He was completely right. Life was messy, and you were never prepared when love or loss came your way. Both were capable of throwing you off balance and bringing you to your knees. If only there were a manual on how to deal with the *other things* that happened in life...

I froze. That was it!

"What?" he asked, feeling my spine stiffen.

I pulled away and reached for my phone in my coat pocket.

"Kitten, what's happening?" His voice was laden with concern.

"I need to write this down." I couldn't talk before I forgot it. My fingers worked quickly, typing the words onto my grocery-list app, where I stored important information that should never be stored on a list app, like pass-words and doctor's appointments.

James craned his neck to read my screen right side up. "'A Discovery: Love and Other Things'?" he read aloud.

I smiled at him. "It's the title of my capstone paper."

He beamed at me. "It's brilliant, kitten. Just like you."

Epilogue

The University of Luxor is pleased to present our newest lecture series, *Hidden: Unseen Figures of the New Kingdom.*

"THE TWO LIVES OF QUEEN ANKHESENAMUN"

Presented by
Dr. Sanura Taha-Campbell
Associate Professor & Academic Director of Archaeology, Cambridge University

Speaker Bio:

Dr. Taha-Campbell was born and raised in Sunnyvale, California. She completed her Bachelor of Arts degree at Stanford University in Near Eastern Archaeology and History. Her capstone project, entitled "A Discovery: Love & Other Things Found in Tutankhamun's Temple," earned praise from the archaeological community and was further published in the American Journal of Archaeology. She earned her PhD in Egyptology at Cambridge University, with a focus on Mummification Techniques.

She is an active member of the Society of Archaeological Sciences and the British Archaeological Association and serves on the board of the Council for British Archaeology.

When she's not instructing, she can be found on an excavation site with her husband of eleven years, Dr. James Campbell, and their five-year-old daughter, Zara. Though living in a bi-collegiate home, Dr. Taha-Campbell hopes that one day Zara will follow in her footsteps and attend Cambridge University rather than Oxford University, once again proving to her husband that "Cambridge is number one."

Author's Note

Before I get into a capstone project of my own about why I wrote this book, I'd like to give a huge thanks to you! Readers like you inspire me to continue to tell stories, so thank you!

Also, I need to give a huge shout-out to a few who helped create this book: Paisley, Sam, Danielle, Nisha & Brian, Amanda, and Jaclyn. Thank you so much for always having my back and helping me to put out the best possible version of my work.

Now to the heart of why I wrote this book…

Like Kitty, I am a daughter of immigrants. My mother was from Trinidad, and my father was from Bangladesh. Fifty percent of me is Bangladeshi, and according to my *23andMe* report, I've inherited over 87.6 percent Bengali/North Indian genes. My heritage runs heavy in my DNA, yet I've struggled with that identity for most of my life.

Like most kids of immigrants, you grow up trying to balance your home life, filled with reminders and lessons of where your people came from, with your school/friend life, where you just want to fit in.

My father was the only member of his family who moved to America, leaving behind his parents and seven brothers and sisters in Bangladesh. I have only met his family four times in my life, so my exposure to anything *Bangla* came solely from my father. Because my mother only spoke English, my father's language wasn't spoken in our house very often, except on phone calls to back home.

Sadly, when I was fifteen, he passed away from a long and tiring battle with cancer. Much of what you read in the book about how Kitty's father passed is what happened to my father. He had been suffering from small seizures for years, which were falsely diagnosed as spasms from a pinched nerve in his shoulder.

One afternoon while he was in the yard playing with my younger brother, he had one of those "spasms" and it knocked him unconscious. He was rushed to the hospital, and imaging scans caught a small tumor in his brain. We were told that it was too unsafe to operate on it, since there was a high chance that the surgery would paralyze him for life. Instead, we spent the next year down the hole of radiation and experimental chemotherapy. Our family lived in the hospital. I won't go into much more detail about how hard it was because it actually hurts too much to write all of this out.

It all ended with the night that he woke up vomiting uncontrollably. My mother rushed him to the emergency room. After several grand mal seizures, he was pronounced brain dead and taken off life support while my brother and I sat in shock by his side. We watched my mother and her family cry and mourn, as one would expect when a family member dies, but my brother and I were speechless. We didn't know how to react or what would happen to us. Our security had been breached and someone we had depended on to be our rock for the rest of our childhood had left us without ever saying goodbye. Our identities as Mohammed's children had been permanently cracked.

It was heartbreaking to lose such a devoted and selfless father. I remember watching his coffin roll along the belt into the belly of an airplane that would return him to his homeland one last time. He left me, taking what I thought was my only link to Bangladesh with him.

I've accepted that I may never learn to speak Bengali properly or cook the way my grandmother and aunties did (though I try really hard to learn as much as I can through recipes). Although those things are often the conduit to keeping culture alive, they don't define me as a Bangladeshi. I've learned over time and through having children, that cultural connection runs deeper than expected. The pride that I have for my heritage can never be taken away from me. It runs in the blood that pumps through my heart and is embedded into my DNA...the same DNA that I pass onto my children. I am a Bangladeshi American and damn proud of it.

POWER

VICTORIA WOODS

Craving a good mafia read?

Read the first chapter of the book that started it all on the next page!

POWER Preview

Chapter 1

Amelia

BEEP. BEEP. BEEEEEEP.

"Dammit!" I overslept *again* this morning—I had completely missed the first two alarms. If I was late to work, my boss would kill me!

I turned off the third and final alarm, still rattled from being jolted awake, then threw back the covers and ran to my shoe closet of a bathroom to get ready. I could barely move around inside without my legs grazing the toilet or bathtub by accident. The walls were off-white and in desperate need of some fresh paint. I imagined that it was once a bright shade of white, but over time the color had dulled. The grout between the white tiles on the floor was yellow with age and even missing in some spots. Much like the rest of my studio apartment, it was old and cramped. It was outrageous to me that *this* was what two thousand dollars a month could get you in Manhattan, but I didn't really have much of a choice if I wanted to be close to work. The proximity helped whenever I was running late, which seemed to be *always* lately.

I inspected myself in the mirror. The edges were cracked, but I could still see my reflection in the middle of it. God, I was a hot mess! I had stayed up way too late working on code again, and my face showed it. My hair was little more than a tangled auburn nest on my head, and the naturally coarse texture made it difficult to work with on a good day. The bags framing my dark-green eyes nearly matched them in color, and my skin was paler than usual. Even the freckles on my cheeks appeared dull. I really needed to stop working until the sun came up.

Out of time to beat myself up, I quickly brushed my teeth and washed my face. A shower would have to wait until after work. I ran a brush through my hair in an attempt to smooth down some of the frizz, then applied dark brown mascara and nude lip gloss. I threw on a vintage Blondie concert tee over fitted jeans. I took one more look in the mirror, then glanced at the clock and sighed—it would have to do. I stuffed my laptop and headphones into my bag and quickly slipped on my Converse. Then, after locking the door to my tiny apartment, I headed out to face another New York City day.

***

"Amelia! Where were you?!" Just as I'd predicted, my boss was pissed. Jason's face was fixed in a scowl as he stood in front of me, arms crossed over his chest. He was a short man with a thin build and thick-framed glasses perched on the bridge of nose. He was in his mid-thirties, yet his hairline was already receding.

"I'm so sorry. I missed my alarms," I said, apologizing earnestly as I slinked into my chair and unloaded my laptop from my bag. I tried to avoid his frigid stare as I powered up my device, praying that it would turn on faster.

"That's the third time this week!" Jason scolded me without any regard for my coworkers overhearing the admonishment. He seemed to be more irritated than usual today, and I sensed it was more than just my tardiness. "I don't have time for this today," he said as he hovered over my desk, then he placed his hands on the tabletop and leaned in, too close for my liking. "I have a meeting right now. We'll discuss this later." Seething with venom, he lingered inches from my face, and I had to stop myself from gagging on the scent of his cheap cologne.

"Your ten o'clock is here," Tammy, his secretary, announced from behind him. Her voice startled Jason, and he snapped up straight and backed away from my desk, but his gaze lingered on me. I exhaled a silent sigh of relief as the space between us grew.

Behind Jason, I saw two tall men standing outside his office. One was dressed in a dark-gray suit, while the other wore a blazer over a black t-shirt and dark jeans. Their strong features shared a resemblance that indicated they were probably related. Both men had darker complexions and black hair, which made them look exotic. They were both handsome at first glance, but the man in the suit had more of an edge to him. His skin was the color of rich honey and he was taller than the other, though only slightly. His angular jaw had a slight shadow of stubble, which contradicted the rest of his polished appearance. His suit was fitted against his lean and muscular body; it was easy to tell he was in shape from how it clung to his tight body. His full lips were pressed tightly together, as if he were clenching his teeth behind them. However, his hazel eyes were the most noticeable aspect of his appearance.

They were bright and piercing. I couldn't tear my eyes away from their blaze. They stared back at me with an expression so intense, I was almost scared.

Jason turned around. "Ah, Shyam and Jai Sethi. Thanks for waiting." He extended handshakes to both men and ushered them into his office. Before stepping inside, the taller man glanced at me once more. I squeezed my thighs together under my desk in reflex. Then the door shut behind them, extinguishing the fire that had burned a path to my core.

"Oh. My. God. They're so fucking hot!" Natalie was my desk neighbor and friend who had a keen eye for all things *male*. "I wonder what they're here for," she said as she let out an amorous sigh, leaning back into her desk chair.

Slowly letting out the breath that I had been holding during that heated exchange, I replied, "It seems like something serious, judging from Jason's reaction."

"I bet they're the reason Jason lost his shit on the phone the other day. I heard him shout things like 'takeover' and 'layoff' when I was about to go into his office to get his approval for the new implementation feature," Nat whispered like we were high-school girls gossiping during class.

"Takeover?" I questioned. "You don't think they're here to buy the company?"

The startup was relatively small and new. With about twenty-five employees including Jason, IP Innovations wasn't quite as green as some of the other startups out there, but we were by no means a huge force in the tech world yet. We had made a splash on tech blogs with our facial-recognition software, which could track the locations of people photographed by mobile phones. Facial-recognition software already existed but lacked accuracy for faces of women and people of color. The government had their own version of the software, but ours was the first with a ninety-seven percent accuracy rate. We'd formatted it for social media use, allowing platforms like Facebook and Instagram to recognize faces more inclusively. As a result, it would make "checking-in" easier for users and garner more ratings and reviews for local businesses.

Jason had even been interviewed for *Forbes*'s "30 under 30" list as a result. I guess it was expected that a startup could be bought if they produced successful products, but I hadn't been expecting it to happen to IP Innovations so soon. I had assumed that when the time came, a social media company or even the government would buy our feature and implement it.

IP Innovations had only been up and running for about six months. I liked the other programmers I worked with—minus Jason and his creepiness toward me—and the work itself. I liked it so much that I spent hours coding at home, sometimes well after midnight.

I dreaded being acquired by some enormous tech corporation where we would go from being people with names to just employee numbers. Programmers often lost their passion and drive when these mergers happened, since they were no longer a part of a small, close-knit team.

Nat's voice pulled me from my train of thought. "Well, whatever happens, I wouldn't mind working *under* one of those new bosses…or both!" She licked her lips in the most obscene way, probably playing out some sort of orgy fantasy in her head.

I rolled my eyes. "You have problems!" I redirected my focus back to my laptop monitor and started typing out code.

"No, *you* have problems, missy." She pointed a finger in my face. "You're like asexual! You barely even date. When was the last time you even got laid?" Everything was about sex and how she could get some in Nat's world.

"Hey! I *do* date," I protested. "Last week, I went out with that guy from the advertising company next door, remember?"

"Did you fuck?" she asked, raising an accusatory eyebrow.

"Oh my God, Natalie!" I prayed she would lower her voice before any-one else heard what we were talking about. "I'm not telling you anything," I whispered, hoping she would lower her voice to match mine.

Ignoring my hint, she continued at her regular volume, "That's because there's nothing to tell, or you wouldn't be so uptight right now!"

As much as I hated to admit it, she was right. The advertising guy was cute, but I was so bored at the bar with him that night. He kept talking about himself and barely asked me anything about my life. At one point, I gave up trying to participate in the conversation and instead planned out new coding algorithms that I could use at work in my head. I ended the night early and rushed home to code until four o'clock in the morning.

It wasn't like I was avoiding sex. I was not exactly a virgin, but my experience was fairly limited. I had given a blowjob or two and had some "okay" sex with past boyfriends. I hooked up with a few guys when I first moved to the city, but nothing ever lasted longer than two weeks. I had never experienced anything like the stories Nat would share about her escapades. She was a freak and was into really wild sex. The most adventurous thing I had done was give my high-school boyfriend a blowjob in the backseat of his car after we left the movies one night. To be honest, my orgasms came easier when I was left to my own devices—devices like my vibrator.

I found it difficult to find a guy who could understand my personality. I was an introvert, so putting myself out there and dating was not comfortable for me. The guys I did go out with took advantage of my quietness and over-took our conversations. I didn't think I was socially awkward, but I always doubted myself after dates. Maybe I really was the problem? Maybe I was sabotaging my sexual encounters, and that was why they weren't exciting? Maybe I wasn't capable of being adventurous in bed because I was too much of a recluse? I wished I could be more like Nat—assertive and carefree.

Sensing my discomfort, Nat eased up on me. "Come on. Let's take an early lunch and check out that new taco truck down the street. Jason's not even going to know we left," she offered. I was relieved to drop the topic of my sex life—or lack thereof.

To keep reading more about Shyam and Amelia, check out Power!

Other Works

The Power Series:
I. Power
II. Empowered
III. Control
IV. Uncontrolled

Numinous

About the Author

Victoria Woods is an International Bestselling Author who enjoys crafting stories filled with suspense, smart female leads, and sexy alpha-males. Inclusion and diversity are important themes in her books. The darker the romance, the better.

A native Floridian, she now lives just outside of Seattle, Washington. Drinking coffee while creating stories as the infamous northwest rain taps at her window keep her inspired.

instagram.com/victoriawoodsauthor/

goodreads.com/author/show/20896193.Victoria_Woods

twitter.com/VictoriaWWrites

facebook.com/VictoriaWoodsAuthor

www.VictoriaWoodsAuthor.com

www.ingramcontent.com/pod-product-compliance
Lightning Source LLC
Chambersburg PA
CBHW020149310726

48970CB00006B/2076